Praise for *Anomie*

"Readers who want a philosophical, accessible, and involving read that uses the character of a displaced American professor in China to explore these transition points will find in *Anomie* an exploration of the connections between individual and society, all wound up in the microcosm of one man's life and bundled into a story that seems light, but quickly moves into the depths of darkness and out again."

—*Midwest Book Review*, D. Donovan, Senior Reviewer

"With strong, clear prose Jeff Lockwood illuminates the state of moving between cultures, physically, emotionally, and romantically. It's not that his character, Michael, has no connections, or no heritage. And yet, from the age of three, he has chosen to separate himself, to be an outsider even in the places, and with the people, he loves."

—Rachel Pollack, recipient of the Arthur C. Clarke Award and the World Fantasy Award

"*Anomie* is the compelling story of an American professor, who explores the maximum of humanity, while teaching in China. His introspection of personality, psychology, and intimacy serves as his spiritual sustenance and emotional outlet. The story is filled with a hint of hesitation, disappointment, and sentiment, which is by no means just personal lament, but a projection of the disillusionment of reality in the heart of the protagonist. The flow of lost happiness and bitter desire is intertwined in the sentences so wonderfully crafted by author Jeffrey Lockwood. Anomie is a confession of love for life, and of identity, in turbulent and mutable societies."

—Cherish Liu, coauthor of *Zi Liu Ji,* a collection of bilingual poetry, Heilongjiang University Press, 2012

"Within the pages of *Anomie*, author Jeffrey Lockwood contrives the life story of Michael, through his search for self-fulfillment and a sense of belonging. His journey leads him from the U.S. to Ukraine and China. His eyes study the people around him. Their pasts and futures intersect with his. But, these places bring him only restlessness and alienation, as one could assume from the novel's title. Anomie is an ingeniously crafted, intriguing novel about one man's search for his own sense of place, and the place where he belongs."

—Angela Wang, M.A., scholar of English language, literature, and culture

ANOMIE

by

Jeff Lockwood

an·o·mie

noun \ ˈa-nə-mē\

: social instability resulting from a breakdown
of standards and values; *also*

: personal unrest, alienation, and uncertainty
that comes from a lack of purpose or ideals

Merriam-Webster
m-w.org

For Angie

PROLOGUE: THE STORY

FRENCHIE HELD MICHAEL firmly against his chest and rocked. He softly told Michael the story of *Gookoosh*:

"*Gookoosh* left 'is place o' birt', journeyin' far t' find *naboob*. Soon 'e come t' a place, a very strange place, wit' a strange language, an' a strange custom, an' e'eryt'ing was crowded toget'er an' built upon itse'f . . ."

And, as he told the story, Maud stopped putting away the leftovers and listened. When he finished, Frenchie whispered to Michael, who was now fast asleep, "T'is yer story, my li'l *goret*, an' yer very own."

Maud finished washing the supper dishes, and walked in from the kitchen. "I really need to record your stories, Frenchie, for Michael's sake, so he'll have them when he's grown," she said, softly.

"What? No. We don't need no et'nologist in t'e family. Michel, 'e'll learn t'ese stories from me, t'e proper way. I make sure o' t'at. T'ere's plenty o' time fer all t'at."

"But, it would be more reliable to record them. That way they wouldn't be lost, if something were to happen. That's how an *educated* person would reason it," said Maud, condescendingly.

"I swear, you foolish way o' t'inkin' is gonna be t'e deat' o' me, Maut. No recordin's and t'at's t'at," snapped Frenchie. He kissed the top of Michael's head and whispered, "*Bonne nuit*, my li'l *goret*," and handed him to Maud to put to bed.

PART ONE: THE TRAIN RIDES

MICHAEL

ON THAT PARTICULAR DAY in early September, the morning broke unseasonably cool and overcast in Jinan City. Michael and Li Qin stood on the platform and said their goodbyes. He would return to Harbin, to the language institute; she would stay in Jinan City, where she taught English at an elementary school.

The whistle blew.

"I've got to board," said Michael, softly.

They held each other for a moment, quickly kissed one last time, and then he entered the car. There were no tears.

Li Qin waited, shivering. Dressed for the weather of the day before, in only white sandals, knee-length, blue denim shorts, and a yellow sleeveless, cotton T-shirt, she watched the train pull away.

Michael slept all the way to Beijing.

There was a four-hour wait in Beijing, before he could board the train to Harbin. Michael sat at a corner table for two in a near-empty, nondescript dumpling restaurant—the kind with the menu on the wall, replete with misleading pictures of dishes. The restaurant was a few blocks from the train station, where prices were lower. Sipping tea, Michael reread the last few chapters of *Women in Love*. He considered it Lawrence's finest literary work. But of all of Lawrence's novels, he was fondest of *Lady Chatterley's Lover*, and thought it his best story.

The train from Beijing to Harbin was crowded and stuffy. Passengers packed the aisle. Some sat on small, folding stools. Others stood, either propped against one another or the backs of seats. The chatter was deafening, like the seasonal migration of snow geese. An old Chinese man sitting across from Michael lit up a cigarette, even though it was prohibited within the seating area of the cars. He then offered one to Michael, either out of etiquette or possibly to form a bond of solidarity. Michael declined by waving his hands horizontally back and forth and saying, "*Buyao xiexie*" (no thank you), even though it was considered rude to decline an offer. But, he didn't want any potential hassle; Michael hated being publicly chastised by so-called officials, and really anything else that might call attention to him (*hey, look at me, the stereotypical, stupid foreigner!*).

Presently an argument in the aisle ensued—it had something to do with the placement of travel bags on the overhead rack—which quickly turned into a shoving match. The car grew silent, momentarily, as everyone turned to see the fight and quickly snap photos of it. Michael kept vigilant; would he know if something were about to turn threatening? Each man presently had the other by the throat, and both were gurgling and turning red, when suddenly a woman screeched something in Chinese. The men immediately stopped and took their seats. A conductor stepped into the car, looked around for a quick moment, and then exited via the same door he had entered. Remarkably, during the course of the official's entrance, the problem had been solved. One man offered the other a cigarette, and they smoked together. Wow!—thought Michael, I think I've just witnessed Chinese diplomacy at its most rudimentary level. Quickly pulling out his "field notes", a notebook in which he kept some thoughts and descriptions, and a pen, Michael began describing the scene he had just witnessed. It could certainly be used in one of his works-in-progress.

Though he'd ridden trains one summer in America, a few years back, the purpose of those travels was to express his feelings of loss, and to develop self-identity as a way to cope with loss. It was pragmatic, something necessary. However train travel in China was different. It provided ample material for his stories. He had only to use his creative instincts and, since he had no idea of his fellow passengers' lives or their relationships to each other, his imagination could and would run free. And, the changing landscape could always be used as a backdrop. Train travel in China was a creative endeavor for Michael.

The train ride from Beijing to Harbin was a long one; he had purposely chosen one of the slow trains with multiple stops. There would be more local travelers, he knew from experience. And, locals were far more interesting in appearance and mannerisms than 'the new rich', which to him had become cliché. Michael settled back, keeping his pen and pad at hand.

Michael opened *To Have and Have Not* (the sole first edition of a Hemingway novel in his collection), the only other book he'd taken along. But he couldn't concentrate. After rereading the same page three times (he'd read the novel many times before), he shut it and thought about their past weekend together—he and Li Qin's—and the promises they'd made to one another. Would they ever be together again? Would it be in Paris? Michael loved Paris. But did he love Li Qin? Could he trust her to be faithful in Paris? It is Paris, after all, and he had played the fool before. Women had taken advantage of his naiveté, likely more than he knew.

"I'm not quite sure if I want to chance it again," Michael said aloud, to no one in particular. The old Chinese man sitting across from Michael looked at him inquisitively and smiled nervously. He fidgeted. Not knowing what Michael had said, and not knowing what else to do, the old man offered him a cigarette. This time Michel took it.

Detached and alone in his head, Michael's own story was being continuously narrated in third person omniscient; flashes of past encounters vivid before him, of stories read and told, some by his own conjuring, critiques of his thoughts, his motivations, his actions, his performances, time and again self-disparaging: *What is wrong with you, Michael?*—so glaringly real at times, while grossly embellished, absurd and fantastical at others; his mind racing from one thought to the next, and always missing that one, immediate, ever fleeting moment of the present, instantaneously lost in oblivion.

It all began, when he first broke free from Maud at the age of three, and became separate, individual—"Mom, I am me, and you are you"—and then belonging only to the seasons, but removed from them, and alienated from them. He was alone, continuously finding himself on his own.

Burdensome, heavy memories, mouthing (most of the time, without even realizing it) words of past conversations, of contradictory and disjointed arguments, like loop recordings over and again, burned into his consciousness, until they became his other reality (*isn't the past but an indistinct shadow of the truth?*); a non-linear succession, where all was fragmented and randomly organized, but where it eventually all came together, a melding into one; and where it was known and understood, but differently.

Now, Michael was so far removed from home that he tried to remember, though he knew it was much safer to forget.

Michael turned to the window. But the landscape remained unchanged for miles, and he grew restless with its flatness and emptiness. Only scattered villages, some virtually vacated, every now and then, came into view. He knew when the train was approaching a village by white pollution, mostly plastic bags—decaying ghost-like figures, clutching, clinging to the limbs of deciduous trees and scrub brush—becoming increasingly visible. His thoughts drifted back to Crooked River, a small village on the south shore of Lake Michigan, in Michigan's Upper Peninsula. It was Michael's birthplace, an antithesis of the present, rural scene.

In Crooked River at that time of year, the fishers were preparing for winter. Some had already headed south or to the Pacific Northwest to fish. While others stayed put to become carpenters over the cold, dormant months.

What about Loch? He missed Loch. He'd always have something supportive to say. And Ivan, where would he be at this time of year? Was he still alive?

And then Helene came to mind. Always present was Helene. With her gone and Li Qin now in Jinan City, Michael was alone again. It was expected. He had anticipated it. Though familiar, the feeling was never welcomed. There was uncertainty in it (the feeling, that is)—a restlessness of being on his own.

Since Helene, Michael had searched for balance between professional expectations and personal fulfillment, but in the end found only indifference and boredom. Were the two mutually exclusive? In American academia, success was measured by performances. He had certainly outdone himself with awards. *But aren't awards subjectively and arbitrarily given?* Teaching bored him. But, he loved to create. So, his performances were simply teaching, which he loathed, and creatively producing, which gave him immense satisfaction.

Teaching, like so many other mind-numbing duties, had cluttered his thoughts with all those "leeches" (he had come to call them), vying for his time. American academia was contrary to Michael's persona. Thankfully, with him now in China, there would be no more research, or "seeking the obvious in the mundane", as Michael had often quipped.

Although obligated, he desired only solitude in his profession—his quietness inherent, his nature reticent (though, those attributes were most often misunderstood and mistaken for aloofness and silent arrogance). When asked, "What is your opinion, Michael?", when discussing some sort of academic question, it was painfully insufferable for him to show any interest, and he wanted to shout, "I don't have one! I'm bored beyond all measure! Let's find a live band and drink some beers!" But, Maud had taught him to always be polite.

"A hunter-gatherer in a village of farmers", he was once called, but he couldn't remember by whom; it was probably an anthropology grad student, or a burnt-out social worker. And, for the past few years (since Helene's "departure", and to a lesser degree *the* accident), it was even more difficult for Michael to sit still. He wasn't able to concentrate for very long at any one stretch (was it latent ADHD, depression, or simply boredom?).

Seeking balance required change. And, with every adjustment made, Michael wondered: Will this finally be it? So, desperately he sought . . . was always seeking . . . searching for . . .

What?—he wasn't sure. If he didn't know, then how could he ever find it?

China was of little help in the matter. But, there were some benefits to being there, such as ample free time, which Michael used to write. And, professional expectations were far less rigorous than anywhere else on the planet. Still, he hadn't felt satisfied. No, it was stronger than mere dissatisfaction; it was that he hadn't felt self-fulfilled in China, either. Success was best measured by self-fulfillment he had always reasoned, and Helene had been his definition of, and impetus for, success. It was all Helene; and it had been all *for* Helene; she had literally become his better half. Helene was 'perfect' and deserved his perfection in return.

HELENE

WHEN JACK AND DIANE finished their Master of Public
Health degrees at Johns Hopkins University, they were first
married, and then they volunteered for the Peace Corps and
were sent to Senegal. They settled well into their new
community, and were respected by local residents and
international health professionals, alike.

About a year into their two-year assignment, a community
elder, with a girl in hand, came to their office. The child was
the elder's granddaughter. She was 14 years old and pregnant, a
victim of multiple rapes. The elder came with questions and
possible directions they should take. Jack and Diane suggested
adoption over abortion, because of the times, the state of
medical services available, and that the grandmother was a
devout Catholic. The grandmother agreed.

A few weeks passed, and, over that time, Jack and Diane
decided that they would be the ones to adopt the baby. They
contacted the Senegalese and U.S. governments, and began the
adoption process. Meanwhile, they secretly kept the girl in their
home, and nurtured and sustained her.

Two months before Jack and Diane's Peace Corps service
was concluded, the girl gave birth to a healthy seven pound,

two ounce girl of interracial mix—African and Caucasian. Jack and Diane named her Helene Louise.

Helene grew tall and strong and beautiful. She was athletic and intelligent, and had a knack for literature and creative writing (poetry being her forte). When it came time to enroll in college for her undergraduate studies, she chose the best school for her interests, the same one that Michael had chosen for his M.F.A. Acceptance into the program was never an issue for either of them. Both had been widely recruited.

As a young adult, Helene was strikingly exotic. She was dark, though not as dark as most Senegalese, tall and sleek, with otherworldly blue eyes. And, intellectually, she was brilliant. *But, isn't it true, that given the same opportunities, females generally outperform their male counterparts, academically?*

Michael was tall and slim, with broad shoulders and narrow hips, dark brown, thick wavy hair, and light green eyes. The spitting image of his father, Frenchie, though not quite as dark, he was popular among females on campus. And, in academic circles, Michael was called "the up and coming" and "the one to watch". By then, his publishing record had already become substantial. He'd garnered a number of scholarships and fellowships (and other such awards; all with stipends), and many were nationally prestigious, thus creating a rift between him and some of the other less gifted, lazy, insecure, and/or unlucky, underfunded graduate students. Some saw his success as derived from preferential treatment.

It was only a matter of time before Helene and Michael met, and that was all it took.

Helene, like many others, was impressed with Michael, and so introduced herself to him at a faculty poetry reading. At that moment, they both knew they'd be together. It was destined to be, and they became the program's royal couple.

Years passed, and they were finally graduated—Michael with a Ph.D., and Helene with an M.F.A.—and then were married. Jack and Diane approved. Michael was highly recruited, as expected, and accepted a faculty position at a regional university in the Rockies. The university had a nationally renowned English department, and a creative writing program that was consistently ranked in the top 10 nationally. Helene taught poetry courses there as well, as an adjunct professor. After two years, she left academia for a career in the private sector. She found it easier to write, when not teaching. Michael could relate. And, Helene made more money outside of academia. So, it worked well for both of them.

THE CALL

WHEN MICHAEL WAS GRANTED tenure at the university, with a yearlong sabbatical awaiting him, he applied for a Fulbright Scholarship to teach "American Literature in Early Modernism: Experiences of Expats", at the two most prestigious universities in Ukraine. Helene fully supported his decision, and knew he was a shoo-in. Michael had always gotten what he wanted.

Early in the following spring semester, in the dead of winter, Michael found out the result of his application.

"Helene was first to know," said Michael. The old Chinese man, sitting across from him grinned, and reached for his pack of cigarettes. Shaking his head, Michael again said, "*Buyao xiexie.*"

Michael continued: "It's kind of like this: I was in my office, sound asleep—I'm always really sleepy right after lunch—and the phone rang. I jumped up—

"Hello?" Then, Michael cleared his throat.

"Are you okay?" It was Helene.

"Yeah, fine; I'm fine."

"Michael, you weren't sleeping again, were you?" she scolded. "You sound groggy."

"No, of course not, so what's up?"

"I didn't want to bother you, but, being that it's your office hours—it is your office hours now, isn't it?"

"Yeah," he said, through a yawn, "office hours now. You have my schedule memorized."

"True. So, guess what I'm holding?"

"Well, let me think . . . um, your boobs? That's what I'd be holding, if I were there."

"Cute. No, I'm holding an envelope. It's addressed to you." And, in her cute, singsong, melodic way, added, "Guess who it's from?"

"No idea."

"It's from the Fulbright Program." She was giddy. "Want me to open it?"

"Yes, of course!" As soon as she said "Fulbright", Michael knew he had gotten it. The week he had anticipated the arrival of an acceptance letter was highlighted on his desktop calendar. Smack dab in the middle: the date fit perfectly.

He could hear Helene opening the envelope, pulling the letter out, and unfolding it. There was a short moment of silence—she was reading it to herself—and then she squealed.

"You got it, Michael. You're going to Ukraine!" A minute passed. "Michael, are you still there?"

"Yes! I know. I know I got it." He was smiling into the phone.

"How did you know?" She whined, thinking he'd already been informed, but hadn't told her.

"I heard you squeal," he consoled. "And now we need to celebrate."

"Yes, we do. Do you want me to invite a few friends over, for a little party?"

"No, I think we've been landlocked here long enough. Let's go on a trip, just the two of us. We'll take a week. You can get a week off, can't you?"

"No problem. I'll let Liz know immediately."

"Good, let's go some place we haven't been before. You choose," Michael told her. He hated making those kinds of decisions.

"It'll be some place warmer, that much I know," Helene replied.

"Warmer sounds good. And, I'll leave word here that I won't be in at all next week."

"Do you want me to pack for you, too?"

"Absolutely, but pack lightly this time . . . for the *both* of us. 'Lightly' is the key word here." She always over packed, and Michael became her mule in airports and hotels, in and out of taxis and elevators.

"Okay . . ." (Had she finished? It sounded like she wanted to say more, so Michael waited.) Finally, though hesitantly, Helene added, "Um, Michael, I've been reading about French Polynesia lately. Becky's been there, and she says it's great! It's quite an expensive trip, but what do you think?"

"What do *I* think?" He paused for a minute to create suspense, and then said, "If we're ever going to go to French Polynesia, we should do it now. There's no telling what the future holds. We might never again get the chance to go."

And Helene squealed.

"That was our last trip together," said Michael, to the old Chinese man.

Michael had hoped that his Fulbright experience would be therapeutic, in that it would keep him focused and busy, releasing him from the heartache of the past six months.

THE FULBRIGHT

DURING THE FALL semester of his Fulbright to Ukraine, Michael lectured biweekly at the National Academy of Humanitarian Studies in Kiev, and the National Academy of International Studies in Kharkov, on the American poets and writers of the Lost Generation. It was Michael's area of expertise, but he found it too much of a challenge there. The students, considered among the best in Ukraine, were pompous and disrespectful. They interrupted Michael continuously, and disrupted class by coming in late and stomping out early. One student shouted out something in Russian, as he stomped out the door; the class applauded the heckler. Michael, not being proficient in Russian, had only a slight idea of what might have been said. He knew it had to be offensive. And, they even corrected his grammar in English, but most often incorrectly. The faculty present and sitting in the back rolled their eyes and *pfff*-ed at his postulates. It was tortuous. But, true to post-Soviet stoicism (he wanted to blend), or maybe it was the devoted academic hidden deep within him, Michael persevered. Publicly, he took personal responsibility for his ineffectiveness in delivery. But, furtively, he blamed the students and faculty, their cultural quirks and oppressive history (and anything else that might come to mind at the moment), for treating him so disrespectfully.

Christmas holiday arrived for Michael. On December 22nd, he flew back to the States and, while in flight, debated on returning to Ukraine to finish his Fulbright, or staying put to do a little writing. He thought it might be time for another book: maybe a collection of his short, unpublished poems (most were quatrains), or maybe one publishable poem (*that perfect poem, yet to reveal itself?*), or maybe a novella.

Arriving early evening at his home in Terrace, Colorado, Michael paid the taxi fare and a customary, augmented Christmas tip. The cabby had carried Michael's two large bags to the steps, anticipating an exceptional one; though, he was somewhat disappointed. Stepping up to the front door, Michael drew a deep breath and waited a moment before entering.

"Okay," he sighed.

Stepping in, Michael found the house dark and cold, enough so that he could see his breath. He had left a key with Loch, his friend and colleague, and instructed him to turn on the lights and heat, on the day of his arrival. It appeared he'd forgotten.

With Helene gone, the house was colder yet, without her there to greet him.

Christmas was Helene's favorite holiday. The house had always been festively decorated, from the day after

Thanksgiving through the first half of January. (It had always irritated Michael that, on his birthday—January 14th—the house was still decorated for Christmas.) She baked cookies and cakes and even candies—divinity being her favorite and Michael's, as well—for weeks. There'd be get-togethers almost nightly. And, Michael called Helene "Mrs. Dalloway". Casual acquaintances and coworkers were invited over a week or so leading up to Christmas; whereas, only a select few of Helene's closest friends were invited over for the festivities on Christmas Eve, and for her Champaign brunch on Christmas day: eleven o'clock sharp. A person could always tell where he stood with Helene, just by the date of invitation.

Those were Helene's parties (she, the center of attention), and Michael attended and was cordial, but didn't enjoy himself (he, the quintessential wallflower). Mostly, he despised small-talk; Michael could never understand why, if someone asked him a question, he or she wasn't looking for an answer. Minutes later found him standing at the living room picture window, with Loch (if he had shown), watching the bustle of the season. That lasted for about a half-hour. Then, absconding to Michael's study, the two sipped tumblers of whisky and talked about such things as the bowl games.

But, Helene wanted Michael to be more social, yet comfortable, so one year she invited a couple of his other colleagues and their wives. It was disastrous. The colleagues were polemic, arrogant, pedantic, horrifically uninteresting, and socially inept, as academics tend to be.

Helene: "Would you like something to drink?"

Ostentatious Professor: "I would answer that in the affirmative."

Within minutes of their arrival, everyone (including Michael and Loch), avoided the pair of them. It was the least distressful arrangement.

Their wives were pleasant and appropriate, but uncomfortable. So, with their husbands in tow, they left the party shortly after an hour of their arrival. Consequently, none of them were invited back. They probably wouldn't have attended anyway.

Michael walked to the thermostat and turned it up to seventy-two, paused briefly to listen for the furnace to "kick in", and then to seventy-six, before sitting down on the couch.

"How was your trip?" Helene always asked, in her charming singsong, melodic way, greeting him with a smile and a glass of *Pinot noir*.

"Fine," he most often answered with a smile, regardless, dropping his bags at the door. They kissed and then talked, while they finished their wine. Then, it was off to the shower, and they made love through the night, fell asleep entangled, and awoke late in the morning. Michael, always being the first to rise, made them omelets and strong, French roast coffee. While eating breakfast, they listened to NPR and discussed films and poetry, and Helene's most recent poem if she had one in the works. But, she never allowed him to read it, until the poem was finished and in print.

In any case, that's how Michael chose to remember his homecomings. But, Helene was now gone, and his memories of her and them together were beginning to fade and becoming somewhat distorted.

A knock at the door startled Michael back to the present: sitting in the living room, staring at the corner, in which Helene and he had always set up the Christmas tree.

"Come in, Loch," Michael called out, knowing it had to be him.

Loch opened the door, carrying a doubled-up paper grocery bag, with bottles clinking, and smiling big to see him.

Loch was short, middle-aged, and potbellied. He wore round, oftentimes smudgy, glasses. With a bad comb-over (and with hair obtruding from inside his ears, like a Geoffroy's Tuft-ear Marmoset), and a gray, scruffy beard, he looked entirely like a gnome. In cold weather, Loch suffered from chronic post-nasal drip (*SNIFF*). An ever-so slight Irish accent—he was originally from County Kerry—that he had worked so hard to lose, added much charm to his elocution. However, his enunciation at times reverted back to its original approach, when things got lively. And how he loved to sing and play chess (and sometimes that other game), after a tumbler or two of whisky—Jameson Irish Whisky, being his "poison".

"Sorry, Michael (*SNIFF*), the faculty Christmas party went long. There was a wee too much cheer in the room, and Janus got a bit drunk and belligerent, and told everyone to 'piss off', while stomping out the door. You know: the usual, traditional faculty Christmas party. Too bad you couldn't have arrived a bit earlier (*SNIFF*). You could've joined in on all the fun."

"No need to apologize, my friend. And, I wouldn't have been much for conversation, anyway. A little jet lagged, you know."

"Yes, that is a dreadfully long flight. Have I ever told you about my Fulbright to Moscow, and . . . oh, yes (*SNIFF*), I'm certain I've told you that story many times," said Loch. Michael could only grin. Yes, he had told Michael the story at least a dozen times, probably more. But, that was Loch, and Loch had earned Michael's respect and attention.

"Well, yes, jet lag, I know all about jet lag, and I've got just the medicine for that," said Loch, pulling out a bottle of Jameson's, and setting it on the coffee table. And, then out came a bottle of *Pinot noir*.

"I know by tradition that you'd have a glass of *Pinot*, whenever you'd return from a trip. So, I brought this bottle, as well. I don't know much about *Pinot*—I hope it's a good one. In any case, which would you like to start with? Becky's at her sister's (*SNIFF*), so we've got all night."

"You're not Helene, so I'll get the tumblers," said Michael.

"I trust that means whisky. Good choice, lad," said Loch, opening the bottle.

There was camaraderie there, between the two, and it likely had something to do with latent tribalism.

When Michael joined the faculty, Loch was the department chair and instrumental in recruiting him. A competent administrator, the department—still young at the time—grew and flourished, gaining national recognition and ranking under his tenure. The epitome of a true academic, just being on campus—any campus, for it mattered little which one—

brought out Loch's very essence. But, make no mistake, in academic circles his reputation preceded him; he would always be at the best of schools. Loch was in consideration for the deanship of the College of Arts and Letters at Stonington, to be vacated in the fall. Most figured he was a shoo-in for the position.

Loch mentored Michael. But more importantly, he exemplified contentment and security, knowing what he had to, *and could*, offer academia.

Even more than his mentoring, Loch was Michael's one-and-only trusted friend, a giving and honest man. His wife Rebecca, or Becky as she preferred to be called, was 10 years his junior, and a close friend of Helene's. The four of them had socialized often and traveled occasionally.

Most, but not all, other faculty members were cutthroats, saboteurs, and generally nasty, self-centered, and/or narcissistic bastards, as Michael often said. He could list all their afflictions, individually, even without a DSM IV (Diagnostic and Statistical Manual of Mental Disorders, 4th Edition). They had succumbed to disappointment with their short-lived and meager successes, amongst the ever-present vacillating doldrums of academia. And, then added to that was their alcoholic wives, who were forever flirting with graduate students. It couldn't get any better, would never *be* any better, and so they became complacent with it all. Michael couldn't relate. For them, it wasn't so much about making oneself look good; it was more about making others look as bad as they, or preferably worse. Michael couldn't understand how such behavior could define one's level of success; that is, "If I can make you appear less competent than I, then I will appear more successful than you." Except for mandatory gatherings, Michael tried to avoid his colleagues altogether.

"I have an idea for a story," said Michael, moving a knight.

"Go ahead, mate, pitch it," said Loch, countering his move.

"Well, let me see: I wrote this cheesy love story when I was—

"We all did, lad. Lose it." There was a slight pause, as Loch sipped whisky, and studied the board. Then, he continued, "Describe the protagonist, our hero in one word."

"I'd rather the protagonist not be a hero, but a loser."

"A loser at first—yes!—but our hero in the end. It is necessary. Our hero must face the antagonist, and then defeat him!"

"Why? Why the recipe? It's too restrictive. 'Make it new'!"

"Why do you make things so difficult, Mr. Pound?"

"Okay, okay, our hero is disgruntled."

"That'll work. Now, his—it *is* a 'he', I presume."

"Yes, he's a 'he'."

"In one word, what's his goal?"

"Identity," said Michael, moving a rook.

"Okay, it'll do. 'Identity' is always good, but make sure it's not *banal*, as you just said." Michael chuckled.

"I didn't *use* banal. 'Cheesy' was the word I used."

Loch smirked, and then said, "Next!—conflict, in one word."

"Lost!" blurted Michael immediately, and then chuckled.

"That's quite correct, lad. You've just lost: 'Checkmate'."

Loch raised his glass in toast, and Michael followed. Together they downed what was left in their tumblers, in one gulp each.

"Okay, mate, when you've finished the manuscript, send it to me," said Loch, adding, "Now, let's finish off this bottle, and move on to the next." And, he poured their glasses nearly full to the brim.

The evening ended the following morning, and, for two more days, Michael was left alone in the house. There was no one with whom he wanted to spend Christmas, except possibly Maud—they had become closer during the past year (well, maybe a *little bit* closer) through phone calls—but she was in Aruba for the holidays.

And, did he really want to be physically near Maud—within that sphere of hers? Regardless, it was a three-day road trip from Terrace to Crooked River, over icy roads—too risky. Crooked River was better left for summer.

Michael tried to read but couldn't focus, tossing each book to the other end of the couch, until the pile spilled over and onto the floor. Neither television nor the internet could hold his attention. Nothing could distract his memories of past conversations, and the things he should have said, but thought cliché, so never did.

Out of sheer boredom, all the while, he drank ceaselessly. There was too much downtime. He didn't want to remember, anymore. It was Christmastime, Helene's favorite holiday. She wasn't there, and he was alone.

Christmas day came, and, that evening, Michael decided to return to Ukraine the very next day. There really wasn't a reason to stay any longer, and why had he come home, anyway? It wasn't home anymore. It was more like a crude shelter hastily erected to wait out a day-long, cold drizzle, now that Helene was gone. Their past conversations, her thoughts, the sound of her voice, that big, big smile—

So, Michael packed his bags.

He sat bored for hours, in the quiet of his empty home. His Fulbright experience was, without any exaggeration, a complete and utter disaster. Was it Ukraine? Was it the universities, at which he chose to teach? Or was it him? Had he reached that place in his professional life, where so many before him had surrendered to apathy, the path of least resistance? Was it his time to call it quits, and find something else to do? He had already written off his Fulbright as a waste of time. Was it time to write off academia altogether? Uncertain of his future, angst besieged Michael.

Two days after Christmas Michael arrived in Kiev. He packed up some of his belongings, shipped home a few things he thought necessary to keep, gave away the rest, and instructed his Ukrainian liaisons that he was going to be traveling by train that semester. And then, true to his predisposition, Michael embarked on his travels, all the while embracing the enduring Soviet religion and social construct of vodka and other such spirits. He thought it the best, most effective and enjoyable way to adopt the culture, in the shortest time allowed.

There was very little that he could recall of that spring semester, only his brief visits to a few cities to the south of

Kiev. Berdychiv (an old Jewish trading center, and Joseph Conrad's birthplace) was first, where Michael penned the lines on a paper napkin, in some cold, basement bar: "Berdychiv is:/a muddied path to a hole/in a schoolyard fence". It was after some beers and a couple of shots of vodka, with Ukrainian folk-rock playing and periodically skipping on the CD player behind the bar. Then it was on to Kirovograd, a one-night stopover. But, he did take a long walk along a busy, commercial street. In his "field notes", he had written: "A nondescript city; pig-like grunts from passers-by—'How do they know I'm American?'" After Kirovograd, he traveled to a few smaller cities further to the south, whose names he couldn't pronounce, and had thus forgotten. But, there was one entry on an otherwise blank page in his "field notes", dated 4/20: "What's with all the uneven steps everywhere?" He couldn't remember where he had written it. (Uneven steps were ubiquitous in Ukraine.) And finally, Michael traveled to Nikolayev, where he met Ivan and Natalia in late spring.

It was a warm, sunny morning in Nikolayev. Michael sat alone on a bench in *Kastan Skvier* (Buckeye Square), drinking one bottle after another of cheap, warm beer (Yantar); he was watching people—young women with small children in hand, old women toting faded plastic and cloth bags stuffed with cabbages and potatoes, and the occasional group of rowdy boys with demure girls—milling about and through the park.

Off a short ways, near the far end of the square, old men gathered around a few others, who were playing a board game (not chess, but that other one). Michael could only see the crowd standing around the table, and could only hear the cheers and jeers of every move. He pulled out his "field notes" from his man-purse (a canvas satchel that he had bought at one of his earlier stops) and jotted down: "Here's one thing left to say: I want to learn that game, the one the old men play in the park, when the weather's good like today, in a crowd that's always there, with unruly emotions. I want to learn to play the accordion. Maybe even buy me a *kepka*."

Michael glanced up.

Presently a pregnant woman walked by—it was the second time she had come by that morning, but from the other direction—carrying a bag from the *renok* (large open market). There were more than cabbages and potatoes in it. Michael assumed that she had butter, cheeses, sausages, maybe some dark chocolates, eggs, and most definitely a loaf of bread (that dark, heavy kind). She touched her belly (did she feel a kick?) as she passed. Two surly drunkards across the walkway, and sitting beneath and against a tree, took their eyes away from their emptied, prostrate vodka bottles, and the warm beers propped between their legs. Cigarettes burned low between their stained and calloused fingers. They stared at the mother-to-be (did they know her?), with unspoken thoughts: *sliding their hands beneath her dress, up and over her hips, kissing her inner thighs*, like young men, since long gone, in raw, repugnant stories. Those stories were the same ones they had told over and again to other surly drunkards, about other young, pregnant women. And, they laughed openly, loudly, brash, wanting everyone within earshot to take notice. But, in the end, they only coughed and hacked.

Michael left the park for a beer tent, or any shady place, though really only to stretch his legs and urinate. Passing the old woman on the curb—the one that sang her own renditions of traditional Ukrainian love songs, the same ones from the day before—he dropped some pocket change into her metal bowl.

After he left *Kastan Skvier*, Michael found a suitable, nearly empty beer tent on *Sovetskaya*, a pedestrian street in the city center, to wait out the day. It was there that he met Ivan.

Ivan was at one time a Russian Orthodox priest (and probably still was), with a penchant for vodka and wine. He stood tall and broad, with Jesus hair and beard, preaching repentance in John the Baptist-like fervor and fashion—a long black robe covered his shabby clothes and otherwise unkempt appearance—to prostitutes (were they sex slaves?) and young thugs on the streets, and praying for their salvation. He panhandled, in between sermons, in up-scale shops along *Sovetskaya*, for donations to his ministry. Ivan was homeless, but never without a home. He was welcomed by many people, mostly other priests and Godly people (for "God loves drunks and stray dogs most", someone once said), all over Ukraine. And, where he was homeless, at any given time, depended upon the weather: his migration being seasonal. In springtime, Ivan preferred Nikolayev, though he sometimes wandered as far south as Crimea: Sevastopol, to be exact. Nikolayev was familiar to him—it was the city in which he was born—and the weather was mild at that time of year.

Ivan stopped at Michael's table and asked, in near-perfect English, "Could you spare some change?" Michael was astounded; there wasn't much of an Eastern European accent noticeable. In fact Ivan sounded kind of British.

"Have a seat," Michael offered, and Ivan sat across from him. "Your English is quite good," said Michael, adding, "Though, there seems to be a hint of a British accent there." Ivan smiled.

"I studied at Trinity College for two years," answered Ivan, smiling even bigger.

"May I buy you a beer?" asked Michael.

"If you could spare ten *hryvni*, I could buy a bottle of vodka," answered Ivan, pointing with his chin to a department store on the corner. Michael gave him a twenty *hryvna* bill, and Ivan excused himself.

Twenty minutes or so later, as Michael was finishing his beer and preparing to leave (he was getting hungry, and he'd given up on Ivan's return by then), Ivan returned with a bottle of Ukrainian red wine (Bear's Blood) and sat back down across from Michael. No change was offered back.

Dressed like any Ukrainian man—sporting a new *kepka*, for one thing—Michael asked Ivan, "How did you know that I spoke English?"

Ivan laughed and said, "A foreigner—especially an American—is the only one that looks around, and smiles a lot. Ukrainian and Russian people don't smile in public. It's offensive."

"So, that's why the gypsies bother me so much."

"Learn to scowl, and never make eye contact," Ivan joked. "Or they'll steal your soul."

For three days, Michael and Ivan met at the same beer tent each noontime, and argued philosophies, but never politics (both being apolitical), and the concept of God, and shared their views on literature and women. (Ivan was a divorced Russian Orthodox priest—*how scandalous was that?!*). Ivan, Michael soon discovered, was a true scholar. His intellect was unyielding. He was a man immersed in humanity. On the fourth day, however, Ivan told Michael that he wanted to show him a special place in Nikolayev.

Ivan led Michael to Lenin's Square, through the park to rather long, steep, and arduous (uneven) steps, and to a walkway along the river. They followed the walkway to where steps led up to a bridge that crossed the river, but Ivan tottered down the bank through a narrow, brushy trail that led to the underside of the bridge. There, on a patch of open ground, with a fire pit made from concrete chunks, was one of Ivan's homes in Nikolayev.

Then, Ivan stepped into the brush, and said something in Russian—Michael had no idea of what he had said, or to whom—and out from the brush came Ivan with Natalia, a woman in her mid-twenties, but who looked much older, gaunt and haggard. With long, blonde hair, in an old, frazzled braid, and ice blue, almond eyes, Michael thought that she must have been striking at one time. Ivan introduced them to each other, and Natalia managed to smile and nod a shaky hello. She was weak, and Michael saw in her eyes that she was dying, and there was hope there that she would die soon.

Michael gave Ivan a wad of *hryvni* to buy food and drink for the evening, leaving Michael and Natalia to smile and nod at each other. Any attempt to verbally communicate was futile. And Michael was left to mull over Ivan's existence, his contentedness. *Why was Ivan so accepting of this life of his?*

For years Michael's was a feigned existence in academia, feeling removed—no! He actually *was* removed, too far removed from what was really real. Michael's world had become ever smaller, limited, constricted, sterile, and ultimately unhappy. *But doesn't happiness project lower intelligence?* It'd been stifling; his Fulbright was suppressing. But there, at the campsite at that very moment, Michael felt unmistakably alive again, enjoying what little time there was left (*a life lived is always too short*), and about to celebrate it with new friends.

Ivan returned an hour or so later, with bread, cheese, sausage, vodka, and wine, but again no change.

"We should always seek cause for celebration," said Ivan. And the party began.

The three friends toasted each other continuously, "*Na zda-ro-vye!*", sang songs and even danced to a drumbeat of clapping hands. And, while they rested, Michael told Ivan and Natalia his boyhood stories of hunting and fishing and trapping in and around Crooked River, its sloughs, hemlock knolls, cedar stands, small creeks, and large lakes, all the while with Frenchie. (Ivan interpreted for Natalia.) Ivan told them his stories of travels to London and Moscow, and the many places in between. And, he told Michael about Ukraine, about heroin addiction, HIV/AIDS, prostitution, and children of the road: mostly poor farm girls, who would "go to the road" to prostitute themselves for food, school supplies, a new dress, whatever it was that they needed or wanted at the time. Natalia was a child of the road, leaving a nearby village at 16; HIV-positive by 18; full blown AIDS by 23.

And, when the night turned chilly, Michael built a small fire in the fire pit, so as not to be conspicuous, yet to keep them warm. A few stray dogs stopped by to warm themselves, as well, and to join in the celebration—they too enjoyed some sausages and cheese. The celebration continued until all was spent, and the three bipeds fell fast asleep; the dogs, however, disappeared into the dark, likely seeking another party to crash.

Morning broke cold and overcast; the fire was out. Michael awoke to find himself wrapped around Natalia. She was as cold as the morning. The night before was vague and arbitrary to him. Ivan was gone. *Why did he leave?* A memory of Ivan shooting up Natalia, did he really see that? The only thing Michael knew, at that very moment, with any certainty whatsoever, was that Natalia was dead.

Michael stood up, but immediately fell backwards into a sitting position; his head spinning, throbbing, his body shaking uncontrollably, spasmodically, a sharp pain in his left thigh.

He vomited.

He got to his feet.

He staggered and stumbled his way through the brush, up the bank, and to the street.

He left Nikolayev.

Michael's Ukrainian Fulbright adventure ended shortly thereafter in the city of Odessa, in a bar near the train station, with him doing vodka shots with two Turkish sailors and a rather large, redheaded German woman named Gisela.

Vodka helped. It really did.

(Over the past year, there had been too much pain, too much torment for Michael. There was too much to remember that he needed to forget. With each shot of vodka, or whatever the day's choice was, it became easier. Memories faded, and then disappeared altogether, but only for that day. They were present, when he awoke the following day. So, the cycle was thus continued; it was easier than the alternative: dealing with it, and trying to move on. Eventually, it would be easier, he told himself, continuously.)

Later that day, or possibly the next, Michael met a woman from Venice, and they planned to go to Venice together. But, he woke up a few days later in Strasbourg, in a hotel with only a bed, a rust-stained sink, and a view of a brick building close enough to touch. A woman lay next to him. He was pretty sure she wasn't the one from Venice. She had a tattoo on the small of her back:

A sun in rising

Underneath it a haiku

In Japanese script

And, there was a spent syringe on the floor. His arms were clean, but hers weren't. And neither were her feet. The night must have been a success, though. She was breathing, and he still had his wallet. But, he wouldn't have known if any money was missing. He'd stop counting his cash the year before.

Once outside, and getting his bearings (*Ah—France!*), Michael immediately left for Paris. At Charles de Gaulle Airport, he shared an outrageously expensive, though relatively cheap bottle of wine, with an impassive yet pensively overweight French-Canadian woman.

The French-Canadian woman left shortly after they had finished the bottle, when her flight was called (*good timing*), leaving Michael alone for an hour. (He drank four more import beers—of the four, Czech Budweiser was his favorite.). Alone now, he tried to recall all that he had experienced in Ukraine. It was bittersweet, mostly the former. But, having met Ivan, and finding that one person who Michael could say was truly immersed in humanity, was the trade off for the pain. It had become his Fulbright experience, and Michael considered *that* part of it a real success.

Michael's flight was called, and he boarded the plane for New York. In the air, Michael decided that he would take the train across country, stopping wherever he pleased, staying for as long as he wanted, and living the next few months without a plan.

By mid-August Michael was back in Terrace, apprehensively awaiting the start of the fall semester.

THE ACCIDENT

THE FALL SEMESTER began, and Michael returned to the university. He was even more alone now. Loch had accepted the deanship at Stonington, so he and Becky were already on the East Coast.

In the classroom Michael couldn't focus at all. His motivation was gone. He felt nothing for his career, for his students. Trying to appear excited, with overuse of inflection and gestures, and a fake smile (*sans* smiley eyes), he pretended to enjoy himself. It was a ruse. It wasn't at all convincing. He needed to rekindle the magic he once had, or find something simpler, honest, and far less mechanical to do. But, realistically, academia was all he knew. And, he felt trapped to the point of chewing his foot off.

The following semester, Michael drove north to Saskatoon, Saskatchewan—the largest city in the province, and home to the University of Saskatchewan—for a conference on comparative literature. It was early April, bitter and sunny. A steady headwind, with gusts reaching 50 M.P.H., bucked and tossed his little Chevy S10 pickup truck from side to side, through the flat prairie and farmlands, the entire way. Large tractor trailers sucked him nearly into their sides, as they passed. Michael wasn't sure if he'd survive the drive to Saskatoon. And, what about the return trip to Terrace? *Would the wind subside by then?*

Consequently, he was late for the opening panel discussion, for which he was a scheduled panel member. Arriving with only minutes remaining, he took a seat at the nearest end of the panel, promptly apologized, and tried to settle in to what was being discussed. But, all was a-muffle.

Michael felt strange: he trembled; he sweated; his heart thumped into his throat; he felt a sudden, immediate urge to leap into flight, as though he could soar (he wanted to soar!); breathless; an outburst of sparkles, before his eyes.

What caused it—the wind?

And, at last, when a fellow panel member asked for his opinion on the final topic being discussed, which startled him back to the panel, Michael stammered, "Yes, I certainly would agree,"—it seemed as if the words had come from someone else, from another place, echoing off the walls, the ceiling, the floor; his jaw awkward, heavy, barely moveable; his lips, his tongue: thick; his mouth cotton dry—much to the confusion of the panel. Embarrassingly, some in the audience found it quite amusing.

What just happened?

When the opening panel discussion was officially adjourned, Michael bolted from the stage, and found a bar within walking distance. There, he spent the remainder of the day, partying with a group of university hockey players.

The following morning, he left Saskatoon for Calgary, Alberta. A peer, whom he greatly respected, but was noticeably (and purposely) absent from the conference, taught there. Perhaps a day or two of like-mindedness would revitalize him, he thought.

Mid-afternoon found Michael in south-central Alberta, heading westward toward Calgary, on snow swept Highway 9.

(The wind had subsided considerably, though it occasionally blew a thin sheet of snow across the highway, wherever there was a treeless expanse roadside.)

South-central Alberta landscape was repetitive, flat with farms, small woodlots, and an occasional wetland, thereabouts. Michael was soon dozing off.

"I need coffee!" he exclaimed, though he was alone, rolled down the driver's side window, and turned up the radio (classic country, *what else?*).

Spotting a café in the near distance, Michael slowed and signaled to turn to the right: but then, instantaneously, a deafening BOOM!—metal crunching, an explosion of glass, whirling, rolling . . . silence . . . shouting, mumbled shouts, excited faces, someone pulling at him . . .

"I'm so cold!"

In the ambulance, within a few minutes of arrival at the hospital in the town of Hanna, Michael saw a broken, jagged, bright yellow halo in his field of vision. An indistinct, shadowy figure moved slowly toward him. It came to a halt—

Michael flat-lined. The EMT called it in, and immediately began CPR. By the time the ambulance arrived, the EMT had resuscitated Michael, but his blood pressure had gone through the roof. It was too high to measure.

The emergency crew met the ambulance at the door, and a young, still passionate doctor, whom Michael never got to thank, placed a single, small pill under Michael's tongue. His blood pressure immediately dropped to a safe level.

When he awoke late the next day, still in hospital, but now in Calgary, Michael could recall little, but an apparition of Frenchie standing soberly over him, but saying nothing. He thought he could recall—

". . . standing on an old, dilapidated wooden bridge above a raging, roiling river, so fearful that I cried, and then plunging into it, struggling to keep afloat . . ."

He repeatedly mumbled those words aloud, but only to himself; he was alone in the room, with only catheters, machines that beeped, and a white curtain surrounding the bed.

From that instant, in mid-afternoon, on April 8th, in south-central Alberta, Michael's world was again forever altered. Though his thoughts, and his ability to reason, were unaffected and continued as before, they were considerably slower in coming. Unable to concentrate for more than a few minutes at any given time, it now took weeks, even months, to finish a task that, before the accident, might have only taken a few days of discipline and patience.

Would it ever be the same again?

So, as the months slowly passed, Michael was left with blinding headaches and strange auras, and eventually a codeine addiction.

THE RESIGNATION

IN THE FALL SEMESTER, the next academic year, Michael was again in the classroom. But he'd become ironic. Like an elderly professor waiting out retirement in a year, he had lost his edge, and it was obvious. He didn't care. When asked a question (even a mindless one), he replied, "I'll have to get back to you on that one." If the information wasn't in his lecture notes, right there before him, he couldn't answer the question. He couldn't think quickly on his feet anymore. Students began to complain—first to the department chair, and then to the dean—even more so than is customary and expected. Finally, in sheer frustration, the majority of his students boycotted his classes, and petitioned the university to have Michael replaced.

Michael began to distance himself from the faculty. Continuing to shun faculty social functions as before, but later faculty meetings altogether, he had run the gamut of excuses. There was nothing left to say, but "I want out". He felt obligated to fulfill his duties, though. He hadn't come to the point of resignation, yet.

Then one afternoon Michael had an episode, as he had come to call them. After walking into the classroom, to an attendance of a mere half-dozen students (of an enrollment that neared 150), Michael stood before the class and began his lecture. In mid-sentence, he stopped abruptly, stared unfocused for a few seconds, his face flushed, his heart fluttered rapidly, he smelled blood, and then fell unconscious. Falling backward, he hit his head on the blackboard tray, rolled to the floor, and farted loudly. Though he wasn't physically hurt, except for a small gash on the back of his head, it embarrassed him. And, *that* was the last straw.

From frustration and despondency to self-deprecating and self-loathing, Michael felt worthless. His career had become a waste. He'd become a waste, knowing that he couldn't go on— not at present, anyway. How had it changed so drastically, in just a couple of years? He was too young—still in his thirties— and his career was too young, for such a radical change.

With every falter, no matter how large or small, Michael self-medicated with booze and codeine.

Early one morning, Michael awoke to unfamiliarity: a cold upstairs apartment. He was sitting slumped over on a worn-out, maroon velveteen couch. Two small, genderless Indian children, in braids and white cotton pajamas, stood before him, and Michael asked, "How do I get outside?" He felt as though he was about to vomit. Both children, without saying word, pointed to an old, painted-red wooden door, with a vertical crack down the middle (yellowed, peeling packaging tape sealed most of the crack). Michael hurried out the door, gagging as he went. Once outside, he vomited over the railing, on his way down the painted pink wooden stairs.

Stumbling to a large sugar maple in the parkway, he wrapped his arms around the tree, spun halfway around and thought: I can't breathe. Then he screamed, "I can't breathe!", and momentarily lost consciousness.

"Are you okay?"

Michael sat up and slowly looked up, trying to focus. There, standing over him, silhouetted against an azure morning sky, was Helene.

"What happened?"

"You passed out," she replied directly, but unemotionally.

Michael said, "What's going on? I can't make sense of it—why doesn't anything make sense, anymore?" Actually, he wasn't talking to Helene, but was contemplating the question aloud to himself.

"You're not *the* Michael you're supposed to be, Michael," she said, pausing for a moment, and then added, "Find out who you really are. Search for what's missing within you, and within the life that you've been living. When you find these things, then—and only then—it will make sense to you." She turned and walked away.

Michael sat stunned for a moment, looking at the ground before him, but only seeing the words that Helene had just spoken. He looked up and said, "How do I—

But, Helene was gone.

Thinking it was a curse (*it's got to be a curse!*), he hoped it was an old witch that had hexed him. A curse became ineffectual over time, as the witch grew older and weaker. Or a great distance from the witch rendered the curse powerless. He was told about curses. Old Man LeBlanc had told him about witches and curses. Michael believed in them.

(Was Maud the witch? Or was she the curse? Michael had wondered. He knew that she was oblivious to the power she wielded. It encased her. Those closest to her were the ones most affected. When they were gone from her, she benefited from their absence. Persevering and continuing forward, she subsequently gained more power with each one eliminated. The benefits she collected were the blessings of what remained, thereafter. And, it accumulated.

It was easy for Michael to avoid Maud, and safer, too, to distance himself from her.)

Later in the week, he drafted his letter of resignation. After many attempts to make it cordial, but professional and explanatory, he decidedly wrote: "This letter is to inform all interested parties that I hereby resign from my position as associate professor effective the final day of the present (fall) semester, in order to pursue other personal and professional interests," and then signed and dated it.

Michael walked into the department chair's office with the letter in hand. The chair glanced up from his pile of papers.

"Oh, Michael, good, I've been looking for you. Next semester, it's your turn to offer a graduate-level mini-seminar. Let me know what you propose to do… (flipping through his day planner) by—say—Wednesday, okay?"

"Ah, yeah, about next semester, it isn't going to happen," answered Michael, smiling, though somewhat sadly, and nodding just a little.

"I . . . I don't understand."

"I'm resigning after this semester," said Michael.

"Are you sure?"

"Yes. I'm sure. There's no question about it." And, Michael handed over his resignation letter. The chair scanned it quickly.

"Concise, I like that. And, well, to be quite honest, this will save us a lot of embarrassment, and some legal fees," said the chair, while rereading the letter, and then added, "If you change your mind, and I'm not saying you should, please let me know A-S-A-P."

Michael turned and walked out, not looking back; he was disgusted.

Though he'd known there had always been *some* animosity toward him—professional jealousy, of course, and all those recent complaints by students (*but who listens to students?*)—still, he half-expected some pleading to stay. He envisioned the chair, on his knees, hands folded before him, begging: "Please stay! We can't lose you." But, it was a deceptive arrogance, a false security, hiding behind his minority status, and a façade of past performances. Yet, he would have only snickered and waved goodbye, saying, *"Au revoir,"* as he skipped arrogantly out of the office.

But no!—it was true. Michael had to face the actual and harsh reality: everybody's expendable, even a Fulbright Scholar. And, the truth hurt.

(The Fulbright, as most academics know, is one of the most prestigious awards in academia, worldwide. Only the best of the best are awarded one. The award distinguishes those who rise above and stand apart. For a university—a department, especially—it is bragging rights to have a Fulbright on board. When Loch left the department, Michael then became the English Department's only remaining Fulbright. He thought that meant something.)

It confused Michael, in that he'd been led to believe that it was his awards and publications that distinguished him in academia. Loch had told him many times those exact words. Now, to Michael, it seemed as if he was the only *token* in the department, easy to replace by another token. There were plenty of educated minorities vying for the few positions open to minority applicants. He wondered how the department would recruit for his vacated position.

Wanted: Token Minority Professor/Ph.D. in English/Must physically look like one of the racial minorities in the U.S.A./Send up-to-date 8 X 10 glossy photo (no *PS* please), with a one-page *CV*/No other requirements necessary.

"It's not that I would have stayed—I wouldn't have. But, it would have been nice to leave feeling a little more appreciated," he told a puzzled, elderly custodian, while on his way out of the building.

So, Michael left campus and headed straight for the bars.

(At about the same time he resigned, his neurologist abandoned him—"There's really nothing physiologically wrong with you, Michael"—and then referred him to Mental Health (*yeah, right, like that's going to happen!*), and discontinued his prescription for pain relievers. So, Michael hit the streets for codeine and OxyContin. In between times, he experimented with a mixture of OTCs, anything that caused drowsiness, and slowed things down a bit—cough syrup, Benadryl, Sudafed, and P.M. pain relievers, which he gobbled like M&Ms—mimicking the effects of codeine. Presently, a new addiction emerged. But, the replacements caused 'new and less pleasant episodes', as Michael sarcastically called them: momentary thoughtlessness, sensations of taking to flight, and raging blood pressure.

Then, one morning, Michael awoke to the right side of his face drooping substantially (*Bell's palsy? A stroke?*). He stopped the OTCs immediately, and returned to an old standby: whisky. Though no longer able to afford Jameson's, he replaced it with Wild Turkey—a cheaper, but as-effective substitute. Now, Michael was back within his comfort zone.)

Michael had essentially resigned at the moment he'd handed in his resignation letter. The remainder of the semester he used all his vacation time, personal days, and sick leave to go fishing and hiking, taught a day or two a week, and still collected his paycheck without penalty. Besides his earnings, there was a life insurance settlement, savings, and retirement investments. It was adequate. He could put his house on the market later on. By budgeting conservatively, he figured the money would last two years or more. He'd spend that time writing. And, afterward, he'd move on. That was his plan.

So, Michael enjoyed nature during the day, and at night he drank whisky and sometimes beer in the bars and parks adjacent the campus—anywhere he could find live music, a drum circle, or a group of artists, poets, or writers hanging out and celebrating.

And, that's where he met Geri, a twenty-something part-time college student, who owned a doublewide a few miles out of town, where she kept horses, chickens, and an unremittingly flatulent potbellied pig named Winston.

THE RANCH

GERI WAS WILD and attractive, in a cowgirl kind of way. The stereotypical mesomorphic body type of ranch girls, she covered herself with the conventional ranch girl attire: blue jeans, T-shirts, flannel shirts, a cowboy hat, and cowboy boots. Her long, blond hair was usually kept in a braid, and her brown cow eyes were almost always covered with dark aviator glasses, unless she was in a dark bar. Geri was proficient at drinking. Michael thought he had found his soul mate.

Michael vacated his house near campus, making a break from his past, and moved onto Geri's ranch. There he embraced a simpler, back-to-nature lifestyle, working mostly as Geri's ranch hand. She appreciated his strong back and kept him busy. But, he also did some odd-jobs, like roofing and remodeling to help out one of Geri's exes. He enjoyed doing a little carpentry.

Michael's room was in an outbuilding. It measured 10' X 10', with only a bed and no windows. That's where he slept most of the time, though occasionally he slept with Geri. They were part-time lovers, but she had many others, Michael soon discovered.

"She liked men" in the vernacular, which was a polite way of saying that she was a slut. Michael was forever walking into the kitchen for his morning coffee to find Geri's latest sleepover (sometimes drinking coffee out of Michael's mug, and wearing his slippers), sitting at the kitchen table. And, more than once, the sleepover was one of Michael's former students. Geri always introduced Michael to them as her "hired hand", and Michael nodded and exclaimed, "Well, shucks! Howdy, there par'ner. It's a darn-tooting pleasure to make your acquain'ance, I reckon, a-yuk, a-yuk," or words to that effect, and offered his hand.

With time on his hands (and ample time to sit and think), Michael began to write creatively again. Little else mattered to Michael, certainly not Geri's promiscuity.

As a high school student, Michael's poems were published in local and regional publications, and two in academic reviews. As a college student, especially while working on his M.F.A., Michael's poems found their homes in some prestigious national and international publications, and a few academic ones. It all changed afterward, much to his disillusionment, when Michael became a so-called scholar. But, he didn't want to be a scholar; he wanted to be a writer. And, it became distressfully evident to him that one, after all, couldn't be both. At least he couldn't. Multitasking wasn't one of his strengths. To him, drinking and driving, while smoking and listening to music, was as close as it got for him.

But now, at Geri's, maybe, he could focus on producing again. He experimented.

Michael's schedule was thus: in the morning, he fed the chickens and horses (Geri fed Winston), and cleaned out the pens and pasture, if needed. Then, he read for an hour or two. After lunch, Michael sat at a small redwood picnic table on the deck and began to write, with a tumbler of Wild Turkey and a pack of smokes within reach.

Experimenting with content, in short, sometimes Imagist-like form, Michael created poems from stories that Frenchie and Old Man LeBlanc had taught him as a child, like: "The Fisherman"

> Osprey, once a boy, alone and away he sang.
> I wait for springtime, for the river
> to run rapid, for the osprey to return.

A poem about environmental consciousness, it's from a beautiful, simple little story of how a young boy, through the traditional teachings of his grandmother, saved his village from ecological disaster. But, in doing so, he gave his own life: a willful sacrifice. It's narrated by the grandmother.

(Michael missed Old Man LeBlanc's stories most of all. Not all were the ancient ones that he wanted Michael to know and pass on. Some were simple stories of his daily life, absent of the so-called essential element of conflict found in western storytelling:

I was in the garden, thinning beans, and I saw a bright green worm on a leaf. It lifted itself, and a sparrow swooped down and landed on the nearest beanpole—I could have touched it, it was so close——; it snatched the worm, and then it flew off, into the trees.

Frenchie nodded at the end of the story, mumbled something indiscernible, and Michael was left in wonder—*what did the story mean?*)

Those poems, from stories of his childhood, gave Michael the most satisfaction. They were his art, his expression, and written only for himself; expressing himself was gratifying enough. And if ever again he submitted his works, Michael vowed to use pseudonyms, thereby severing all ties that might bind him by name to academia, desiring only to disappear from a past that he now chose to forget.

It was Michael's celebrated liberty. Who knows?——in 400 years, his pseudonyms just might become household names, he sometimes quipped. Though Geri couldn't understand why he wasn't interested in immediate recognition and compensation.

But, as autumn approached, Michael interests in writing (especially poems) waned. He grew antsy, and became distracted and unmotivated—*why?* He wasn't sure. Putting his thoughts into words was painstakingly difficult. For hours he sat, with his tumbler of whisky and a pack of smokes on the table before him, pen in hand, staring at a blank sheet of paper. Books—his favorites, and even some of his own publications—could not inspire him. Walking did little to help. Writer's block?—*okay, call it writer's block*—but, it probably had more to do with the unsettledness of where he was, and whom he was with. Or, it was autumn, the time to prepare for winter. He needed purpose; he needed to restore balance in his world.

"Why am I still here?" he asked himself one day out loud. He looked around at the ranch, and it—the buildings, fences, stock, Winston, the horse chestnut tree—yes, all of it, appeared so ridiculously irrelevant and mundane. A dry wasteland, he thought. Even the air smelled dry. He missed the smell of wet earth, the way Crooked River smelled. He needed to find that place again. No wonder he couldn't write anymore; he was an alien there.

Sitting at the kitchen table one day, while Geri "went missing" (cruising the bars, Michael assumed), he counted his money. It had dwindled quickly, much quicker than if he had been working, and making the same amount. *How does that happen?* Soon, too soon, he'd be broke. He knew he had to try something different. But, Geri couldn't know; she'd kick him out immediately. He knew she wanted him there, needed him there for the hard, physical labor that she wouldn't do, and the occasional "roll in the hay", but that was about it. Geri wasn't Helene.

Now was the time to formulate Plan B, an answer to the writer's clichéd question: "How can I earn enough money to live on, and yet have enough time to write?"

A few days later, Michael drove into the city to buy chicken feed at a Sinclair's, and afterward stopped by The Blind Pig, a local pub and favorite among artists and writers in the community. It was early afternoon and the pub was nearly empty. Sitting alone at a small, round table was Leon, one of Michael's former M.F.A. students, two-years since graduated, working on a pitcher of beer. Leon saw Michael belly-up to the bar, and so walked up to the bar to greet him.

"Hey Michael, what's up?"

Michael looked into the bar mirror, turned, and grinned, "It's good to see you, Leon. How are you?"

"Good!—yeah, I'm really good. What's this I hear? You quit teaching?"

"I did. Resigned last year."

"Why? So, what happened?"

"I just couldn't do it anymore. Let's grab a table," said Michael, tilting his head toward the tables before the stage.

"So, if you're no longer teaching, then what are you doing?" asked Leon, as they sat down.

"Care-taking a small ranch, and . . . well, trying to do a little writing, but ideas are getting harder to come by lately. I'm not sure why. So, what about you?"

"I just got a story accepted by *North Shore Review*. That's why I'm in 'The Pig'. It's like you used to say: 'Got to celebrate your successes!'"

"That's true. Congrats. I've always thought you're a good writer," said Michael.

"Ah! You just called me a good writer!"

"Oh, geez, sorry!—you're a good storyteller. That's what I meant to say."

"Thanks. Ain't no grammarian, you know," said Leon.

Michael laughed, recalling his rant, in a short fiction workshop: 'A well-written story is not necessarily a good one. That's one reason why we have editors. A good editor knows a good story, and he or she will make it better. But crap, even well-written crap, will always be crap!'

"So, what else is happening in your world?"

"I'm just back from China," replied Leon.

"China? What have you been doing there?"

"Teaching English."

"Teaching in China? Why? I guess what I mean is, why not teach English in . . . I don't know . . . Nebraska, or maybe the Virgin Islands?"

"Nebraska *or* the Virgin Islands?" Leon laughed. "I don't think I've ever heard those two mentioned in the same sentence before. Okay, well, I'll tell you, it's like this: adequate pay to live on, and—

"Taxes have got to be outrageous, communist country and all," said Michael.

"Why do people think that? No, not at all—virtually no income tax. Last year I paid one-tenth of one-percent monthly. It was a flat-rate," replied Leon. Michael stared in disbelief.

"So, your departure . . . did you have a falling out with America?" Michael asked.

"You mean like: 'America, love it or leave it'?"

"Yeah . . . something like that."

"No, not at all, it's more like what Edmund Morris said, 'America, love it *and* leave it'. After I graduated, I taught for a year—back home, back in Kansas—at a community college. But, I was so busy that I couldn't find the time to write. I desperately wanted—no! I *needed* to write, but it just wasn't going to happen." Leon paused to finish his glass, and to fill it again. Then, he continued, "And, I was always broke. My student loan payments were a substantial part of my income, and cost of living day-to-day left me with a choice every month: do I pay my bills, or do I eat? There wasn't the transition from ramen noodles of grad school to real food of a professional career. Where's the reward for all the hard work? I had to sell my car! Actually, that's the best thing that could've happened to me. I didn't realize it until later. Anyway, none of it's a problem anymore, now that I'm in China. I'm living in the shadows, I guess you'd say."

"So, you're going back, huh?"

"Absolutely, there's no question about it; in a few weeks, in fact. Already got my ticket, and now I'm just waiting on my visa."

"Okay, so how'd you find your job?"

"Lots of sites, literally thousands of jobs . . . oh no, wait a minute; Michael, you're not thinking about teaching in China, are you?"

"No . . . maybe . . . I don't know . . . who knows?"

"You've heard about the stigma, right? You'll be a member of the "Loser, Boozer, and Cruiser Social Club", whether you want to be or not, and called a bunch of other nasty things, mostly by other Americans in China. It's weird! They'll question your motives, and, because they're such losers, they'll think you're one, too.

"Go back to the U, Michael. Students need you there. You were such a good teacher, when we had you. I mean, everybody liked you."

"It's not about teaching. It's all about producing."

"I know, but those lazy bastards—

"You're talking about my esteemed, former colleagues?"

"Yeah, they'd be the ones. They're either crazy or lazy; they're terrible teachers. And, when's the last time any one of them was published? It's like they retired once they made tenure."

"That's very true, but it's not about them. It's about me: *I* couldn't produce there, not like I used to. I was just too busy all the time." Michael paused for a moment, and then added, "Damn, I miss grad school—

"But, you must've been busy in grad school, too, right? I was."

"Busy?—yeah, I was busy, but busy doing my own thing. I had a full-ride, and . . . no!—that's not true—I was on *two* full-rides, simultaneously, with absolutely no duties."

"Whoa!"

"Whoa is right: one from the state regents, and the other from the university. Scholarships, fellowships, all sorts of other academic awards, too—virtually all with stipends. God, I was hated," Michael laughed. "Anyway, it's all on my *CV*, somewhere in a box, somewhere in a barn, a little west of here . . . unless mice have made a nest of it. Ironic, isn't it?"

"Why so many awards?"

"They kept on a-offerin' 'em, and I kept on acceptin' 'em," answered Michael. Leon chuckled.

Michael continued: "When I was a grad student, I . . ." He stopped short. He hated the dreaded "used to" verb, used far too often by has-beens. Michael continued, "I need to find that place again. Maybe China could be that place."

Leon looked horrified, as if wanting to say: 'Sorry I even brought it up. Rewind! Rewind!', but only said, "China is but one place, Michael. There are lots of others, and right here in America at good schools. Have you talked to Loch lately?"

"No, I haven't. And you're right: there are a *few* good schools in America. I'm just not sure if they'd be any different. That is to say, would it be the same for me there, as it was here?"

Both sat quietly for a minute, and then Michael said, "Please don't say anything about our conversation today, okay? Chances are I'll do nothing. I'm bored. And, I've been feeling a little unappreciated lately. I guess I have been for years . . . since Helene, anyways."

"Sure, mum's the word." Leon knew better than to push the Helene-thing—he'd heard the rumors.

When their tongues tired, they finished their beers, and said their goodbyes. Leon stayed at The Blind Pig to wait on a friend, and Michael returned to Geri's.

But, Geri was out.

Michael immediately began a search for teaching jobs in China on the Internet. Leon was right: lots of jobs. He clicked on a few of them, and found that they were all about the same: 16 hours per week . . .

Michael leaned back in the chair and sighed deeply. This might be what I've been looking for, he thought. It's been good for Leon. It could be good for me. "But don't rush into anything. Think about it for a while," he cautioned himself out loud.

In early December, Michael was again searching the Internet for teaching jobs in China. After applying for three jobs, within three days, Michael had a solid job offer from Heilongjiang Foreign Studies Institute in Harbin to teach 12 hours of oral English and four hours of American literature. The offer included free housing, utilities included, free lunches at any one of four dining halls on campus (during the five-day workweek), health insurance, travel pay (during winter and summer holidays), and flight reimbursement to and from China. The job started in early March, after the winter break, but the Foreign Affairs Officer at the institute indicated that he should try to arrive a week early. Though apprehensive—he had never been to China before, and, like most Americans, knew very little but skewed half-truths about it—he was excited, as well.

He thought that it could be what he had been looking for: a new beginning. There would be plenty of time to read, to write, and to embrace 'Bohemia'. He would describe the places he visited—as a traveler, not a tourist—the people he met along the way, and the conversations they had had. And, if he could write one piece, just one piece that for him was a clean and honest self-expression—the perfect poem, or a story that had something to say—and be proud to have written it, then he could say, with all certainty, it's been worth the agony of the past few years.

China would be different, Michael convinced himself.

Michael leaned back in his chair and closed his eyes. Then came Helene.

"Are you okay?" asked Helene.

"Yeah, I'm fine. Why?"

"It looks like you're running short of cash?"

"It appears that way, doesn't it?" He sighed.

"It went quickly. Working on Plan B now?"

"I think so. It's time."

"Got a solid plan, yet?"

"Yeah, a change of scene: China."

"China? Yes, that's quite the change of scene. But, a little extreme, don't you think?"

"No, not at all, a clean break is what I need; a totally new perspective."

"Will you teach, as well?"

"Yeah, I'm going to teach in Heilongjiang, 'the old country.' Maybe I'll hook up with some of my lost and forgotten cousins," he said, laughingly.

"You're not talking about the Ewenki hunters and the Nanai fishers, are you?"

"Yeah, those would be the ones," answered Michael.

"That sounds interesting. And, maybe, you'll even find your muse in Heilongjiang."

"That's also part of the plan—can't seem to find my voice, anymore."

"In poems?" asked Helene.

"Yeah, in poems . . . especially in poems."

"It'll come back to you, just give it some time. And, Michael, when you're in China, please don't isolate yourself, okay? You tend to do that, you know. Make friends. Socialize."

"Okay, I'll keep that in mind."

"And, one last thing: I know Geri hasn't been the best for you, but it's important that you take a lover in China. You tend to imbibe at dangerous levels, when you're alone and lonely. With a lover, you'll be more settled. You'll take better care of yourself, and she can help take care of you, too. And, of course, there's that added benefit: sex. It's so healthy."

"Okay, maybe. But, I think it would be easier for me to join a spa and become a vegan," said Michael, laughingly.

"I'm serious, Michael, find yourself a lover, but not one-night stands, like you had in Ukraine and France. Those had the potential of being dangerous, even life-threatening."

"Oh, you knew about those, huh?"

"Nothing you do is left unnoticed, Michael."

HARBIN

MICHAEL STEPPED OUT and into the bustle of the streets in Harbin: "It's so damned cold!", and the cold amplified the noise; heavy hanging, choking, heart-palpitating exhaust fumes; and the looks, the stares, the hacking and spitting, the "ha-rows" (hellos), and laughter as he passed others, and they passed him.

It was early March, and he had just set foot in China.

In no time, Michael had settled quite comfortably into his new apartment on campus. It was large, with four rooms and two balconies, in a four-building apartment complex for foreign teachers, numbering over 50 at the time. He explored the campus grounds (the pond—a pristine enclave surrounded by the noise and remains of development—as Michael had anticipated, became a place of quiet solitude for him).

And, he had begun teaching.

(During his first semester at the institute, Michael taught second-year oral English courses, and American literature graduate courses. Thereafter, he taught only graduate level courses.)

In the first week, Michael introduced himself to his students, and asked them, "Is there anything you'd like to know about me?" He figured they'd ask things like, "Where are you from?" or "Do you like Chinese food?" or "Do you have a hobby?" or something so *thought provoking* as that, and, for the most part, he wasn't disappointed. But, in the last class of the week, a student asked, "Are you married?" It was a fair question in Han Chinese culture, as Michael presently discovered.

Michael answered, "Not anymore."

"What happened?" asked another student, sitting in the front.

"She left me," he answered too quickly, without thinking about it. Immediately, Michael felt nauseous. He excused himself and hurried to the toilet, where he vomited in the sink. Rinsing his mouth and splashing water on his face, he then looked up and into the mirror, and said to his reflection, "Where did that come from?"

Returning to the classroom shortly thereafter, Michael said, "I'm sorry. I don't feel well. Class dismissed," and hurried outside into the bitter cold and quickly lit a cigarette. He asked himself, doubtingly, "Can I really do this?"

Michael was shocked into the reality that teaching in China was absolutely nothing like teaching in America. For one, his second-year students all seemed as if they were 14 years old and very shy. *Had they been beaten into submission?*

(An officemate told Michael, and he soon discovered for himself, a strange phenomenon in China: second-year boys and girls were profoundly immature, when compared to their American counterparts. But, during their third year, there was a great leap in physical and emotional maturity, especially with the girls. By the time the fourth-year students had graduated, they were into full-blown adulthood.)

Rote dominated as the method of learning.

If Michael asked a student a question, he or she would stand nervously speechless, while the entire class answered for the student. No one ever had an opinion or question. And, all agreed with Michael, whenever he attempted to play the devil's advocate.

Michael: Making money is the most important thing a person can do. It's more important than person's health or his family. We shouldn't care about our health or our families, because all of us are going to die eventually, anyway. That's my opinion. What's yours?

Entire class, in unison: Yes, we agree with you.

Michael: No! Our health and families should be *most* important to us.

Entire class, in unison: Yes, we agree with you.

Failing scores (grades), or the threat of failing scores meant absolutely nothing; everybody passed regardless. Students with the wealthiest parents excelled despite aptitude or participation. And, final semester scores were changed without the teacher's consent. Those things he also learned from an officemate, within the first month on the job, and his own observations from thereafter.

A common answer to Michael's question, "What did you do this past weekend?" was answered with, "I played with my friends," meaning "I hung out with friends." Those were students who were 22 years old. (Chinese university students generally begin their studies at the age of 20, give or take.) To Michael, university in China, at the first- and second-year levels, was somewhere between middle school and high school in America, in matters of student maturity and independence. But, to him, at that time, there was something virtuous in his students' mannerisms; in contrast, America, it seemed to him, had grown up too quickly, and had since become corrupted.

From that first week, things slowly began to fall into place for Michael. Within a month, oral English had already begun to bore him. But, there was more than boredom at play. Speaking overly cautious to individual students, and self-criticizing his performances afterward, he felt inadequate as an oral English teacher. It would get better over time; he knew it would have to get better with practice. And practice, he reasoned, would instill confidence in his delivery.

But, in his American literature classes, Michael came alive. It had all come back to him—that necessary façade for him to be successful—teaching in character, where he virtually became someone else (mostly a former professor whom he had admired), while his students remained faceless at their desks. They weren't Chinese; they were only students. Like someone going through emotional trauma, and desperately needing to unload it, Michael lectured to and only for himself; the words came fast and easy. It was a release of what had been stirring within him for years, and it assured him that he hadn't forgotten. He was still competent. And, like a runner after finishing a good, fast 10K road race, Michael was emotionally charged, cleansed; the endorphins had kicked in. Teaching was cathartic.

He talked at length (but admittedly too fast) about early Modernism, and how it had changed the face of American literature forever. It became as much a history course as a literature one, as it should have. Few students shared in his enthusiasm for the subject, but few ever do, and even fewer understood what he was saying. But, almost everyone enjoyed his animated performances. He constantly walked and talked (not sitting, using a microphone, like his Chinese colleagues), his face contorting and his hands flailing. His tall stature and gentlemanly demeanor added much to his delivery. His classes became very popular.

Like a young, arrogant assistant professor, Michael felt confident, lively, and even vital, for the first time in a very long time. And, it showed.

"I really think I can do this," he mumbled, at the end of one of his lectures. Two students sitting directly in front of him heard him and smiled warmly. He had returned to that place. He felt healed. Had the curse been lifted? Was the witch dead? Probably not, reasoned Michael. He had distanced himself far enough from the witch, he figured. Her power couldn't reach him in China.

Michael's professional past—leaving his Fulbright too early and resigning from his faculty position—was never an issue. But, he was uneasy about one thing in particular: it was true that he looked much better on paper than in person. He found that it didn't matter, anyway. Michael was a native English-speaker with exceptional credentials. As long as he looked pearly-white, didn't talk politics (generally teachers were not allowed to speak on the "three Ts": Tibet, Taiwan, and Tiananmen Square), wasn't drunk in class, and didn't have sex with students, everything was "A-Okay". Beyond that, foreign teachers were afforded great freedom in China.

But Michael's colleagues did see him as an enigma, a loner comfortable with only himself. (Unbeknownst to Michael some of the foreign faculty referred to him as "that serial killer in building three".) For one, he didn't discuss politics with them, a norm for new arrivals in China (the *other* opium of the masses, according to Michael). And, wherever he walked, he walked quickly and in deep concentration. Rarely did he make eye contact with anyone.

There were assumptions and then interrogations, and Michael thought little of it at first. He thought his colleagues were interested in him. But, when colleagues asked the same question over and again, Michael realized that they were waiting for him to slip. So, he learned to play along.

"So, why did you leave America for China? There are better opportunities for you there, and it's so much easier to live in America."

Michael answered, "Because it's so much easier for me to live in America," much to their confusion. To his colleagues, Michael's behavior was atypical. Why would anyone with his credentials and experience come to China? And they attributed it to probable deceitfulness (was he on the lam?) or gross exaggerations (he must be a fake!).

And, as odd as it seemed to his colleagues, Michael's behavior seemed even more so to Chinese people.

Students were inquiring: Was he shy, or just a bit odd? When seeing Michael walking on campus, looking at the ground before him, they called out, "Mr. Michael, Mr. Michael, you always thinking." To which he replied, "Don't *you* always think?" He found it peculiar that, in response, they only looked at him amused. He could never tell if that meant yes or no.

But, in Michael's defense, it is the nature of a poet to be in his own mind, continuously searching for that one evasive word that might bring his poem into balance. Michael was constantly walking past his classroom, or entering the wrong building, or showing up on the wrong day. He was lost in his own abstraction.

Avoiding social events and even invitations, Michael buried himself in his teachings, in his own studies of Tang Dynasty quatrains (he'd previously studied them in grad school), and in his writings. There was no past, only "right here, right now", for Michael. His business was of no concern to anyone, anyway. The wall he had built so long before was still impenetrable. In return, Michael remained leery of others' intentions. But mostly, he didn't care, and found it safest just to avoid them, altogether. He was comfortable in isolation.

Eventually, it all settled well for Michael. He figured he could be his true self there, regardless of what others might think. Isolation in China was an easy thing to do. Knowing that language only obligated him to interact with locals—an excessively time-consuming obligation—Michael resolved to learn only enough Chinese to survive. *Comfort leads to complacency, a writer's greatest adversary, for in adversity writers learn to be creative; it's a matter of survival.* Michael's became a reliable and necessary ignorance.

Campus became his temporary Walden, a hermitage of sorts, and his needs were few: a stack of good books (books in the public domain were infinite in China, which worked well for Michael, given his obsession with early Modernism), an idea for a poem or story, and the right woman. But, regardless of location or situation, it had always been that way.

(The only thing he was unsure about was 'the right woman'. *How difficult would that be?* Being new to China he had nothing to compare it to. Who could he ask? Who could he trust? He didn't want anyone to think that he was there for a wife; he wasn't. Those men, like the "wife hunters" he saw and met in Ukraine, were desperate and thoughtless. Ukrainian women were frantic to leave. Divorced, poor, and with children, it was the children that mattered most to them. But, many wife hunters were there only for sex tourism, under the guise of finding a wife—"after all, no one buys a used car, without test driving it first". Many were in China for the same reason. Michael worried that his credibility would be jeopardized, if he made public his interest in dating a Chinese woman. He could use one of the online dating sites, but anyone with Internet access, including his colleagues and students, had access to it. He was lonely, but chose to wait it out to see what happened naturally.)

Spring was late in coming. But, almost overnight, the campus erupted in myriad colors—reds, pinks, yellows, blues, ad infinitum—and from ground level it was Eden. On the commons, fruit and nut trees blossomed and flowering shrubs bloomed. The embankment along one side of the pond was left natural, where wildflowers and grasses and native brush grew thick. There, songbirds—those staying put for the few short summer months, and a few that had stopped for a rest on their way northward—hopped from branch to branch, and called to their mates in the cool air, of the dewy, early mornings of June. A hen pheasant, with her chirping brood, was a daily performance for Michael.

From Michael's sixth-floor window view, Eden was still there and itself—a paradise, within walls. But, the reality of where he was—Harbin, China—was too evident outside of campus. In the not-so-far distance, countless smokestacks endlessly released their poisons into an otherwise azure, morning sky. Plumes transformed the city to a dull, gray glow. An opaque, hazy blanket consumed Harbin. Visibility was less than two miles.

CROOKED RIVER

THE SEMESTER ENDED in early July, and Michael returned to the States for a short visit, and to finish some neglected business in Terrace: he cleaned out the house and garage and packed two travel bags, with what he wanted to save. Most everything else he donated to charitable organizations, though he left most furnishings and appliances in place. Then, he put the house on the market. It would surely sell—its location being a university town—but he was certain to take a loss. He didn't care.

Michael stayed in the house for almost two weeks, but he was lonely there. It had been Helene's house, and she made it their home. But, she was gone now, and the house was quiet and cold, regardless of the warmth and humidity of mid-July. The whisky flowed freely, both night and day. It was time to visit Maud. He knew the risks, but he was running short of money.

Michael opened his eyes. All was a-blur. "Focus!—oh, yeah," he said aloud. It was the ceiling of his S10. He sat up; his head hung heavy, throbbing; his body stiff; a sharp pain in his left thigh. The cab of the pickup truck smelled sour. He smelled sour. On the floor, lay a half-empty bottle of Wild Turkey.

Getting his bearings (*Oh, that's right—Wal-Mart*), Michael stepped out and started for the store's entrance. He needed to urinate badly, and splash some water on his face. Checking his wallet, there was only enough for gas and cigarettes. He wasn't going to eat today. "But tomorrow, I'll be home," he convinced himself. No matter where he lived, Crooked River was Michael's home. It always fit his definition of home most closely.

It was early morning—too early for the store to be busy— and Michael staggered his way through the entrance, and eventually found the bathroom at the rear of the store. A few customers and salespersons stared at him as he passed. But, he was used to the stares now. He knew he looked as badly as he felt, probably worse. But, when Michael saw himself in the bathroom mirror, he realized just how badly he actually looked. "Geez!—I look like some old, homeless guy," he said, disgustedly. Homeless never, but Michael was looking haggard, and well beyond his years.

Back in the pickup truck, Michael sighed big and said a quick, "Please God," and turned over the engine. It groaned for a moment—an old, worn-out battery—but then caught and quickly started. The gas gauge showed a quarter-tank. He tapped it; then, a little more. "Should get me about 100 miles," he said, as he started out of the Wal-Mart parking lot.

Michael grabbed the pack on the dash and felt it. There were only a few cigarettes left. When he stopped for gas, he'd buy another pack. And, that pack would have to last him through the rest of the trip: some 400 miles, give or take.

Pulling out and onto the highway, Michael lit a cigarette and turned on the radio. Driving into the bright morning sun, he searched for a radio station, other than classic country or the farm report.

It was a long day.

Sunday morning the town of Crooked River (population about 600, depending on the season) was quiet and damp from an intermittent, early morning drizzle. Low, ragged clouds and wood smoke hung on the rooftops, concealing the tops of pines and spruces and a few red cedars along the roadway—Main Street. An old, red and white Dodge pickup truck sat cold in front of the Crooked River Bar & Grill, the only bar-restaurant in town, the owner of the truck sound asleep in his bed or maybe somebody else's. Crooked River General Store wouldn't open for another three hours. The Crooked River Building Supply was closed all day. In a few houses that lined Main Street, the only paved street in town, and the five graveled side streets—First through Fifth—kitchen windows shone yellow, in the blue-gray morning light. Those were the homes of Crooked River's Catholics, who traveled some 50 miles to Red Rock for Sunday mass; or the homes of the minority Protestants, who met in living rooms and around kitchen tables of their neighbors; or the unfortunate few whose jobs required them to work every day, without the duly earned and accustomed day of rest. Most of those homes were clapboard, and in desperate need of paint. But paint was expensive, and almost everyone within the city limits of Crooked River was dirt poor.

Michael drove into the 160 (pronounced "the one-sixty"), a quarter-mile square, and original site of the incorporated City of Crooked River.

Continuing down First Street, past where Frenchie grew up, and onto Crooked River Road, a narrow, winding gravel road that followed the course of Crooked River, through hardwoods and wetlands, Michael drove some 15 miles to Maud's home.

He was home now: the familiar scent of wet earth told him so.

Maud was in the kitchen making coffee, when Michael knocked. Susie, Maud's Golden Retriever, barked. Maud peeked through the window.

"Michael!" Maud squealed, as she opened the door.

"Hi, Maud," he said, with a big grin.

"It's so good to see you, Honey," said Maud, hugging him tightly and kissing his cheek.

For Michael, it was surprising how Maud had aged in just a couple of years. The last time he had seen her was at the funeral. She must be 60 years old now, thought Michael, or close to it. He'd forgotten her birth year. Maud's eyes looked tired, like she'd seen too much. The beauty of middle-age had crept away. But, Maud had remained active, and kept her mind sharp.

"How was your trip?" asked Maud, after gaining some composure.

"It was okay . . . long." He felt the sting of hunger. He'd been starving himself for a week', drinking whisky and smoking cigarettes for sustenance. All sensations were amplified, and his movements quick and jerky. His eyes burned and were watery. His breath was foul.

"This is temporary, isn't it? That is to say, you are going back to China, aren't you?" There was an uncomfortableness that Maud felt with Michael being in Crooked River. After he'd dumped his professorship, she was no longer the mother of the "award-winning professor of English and creative writing"; would *she* be judged as a failure?

"Trying to get rid of me so soon?" He laughed. "Of course, I'm going back. I like it over there," he said, pointing with a tilt of his head and a tip of his chin. "It's a new place, a new perspective; it inspires me."

"Yes, I do remember you telling me that poets are writers of place," said Maud, nodding in agreement.

"Yeah, but now I'm experimenting with fiction. I just can't seem to get it right . . . my poems, that is. I don't know what's going on. Maybe, I should study poetry in depth again, and forget about *writing* poems."

"It'll come back to you—all in due time, Honey." Maud poured Michael a cup of coffee, and then added, "Writers write from experience, don't they? I guess what I'm asking is, are you going to write about me?" Maud was concerned that he would put her in a bad light. She had a reputation to uphold in the community. It had already diminished some, with Michael now teaching in China.

"That's not what 'writers write from experience' means, not totally anyway."

"What then?"

"Writers write from observations of the human condition, in all of humanity, and the natural and artificial worlds before them. They find inspiration in good stories."

(Michael had always preferred literary storytelling, and shunned contemporary commercial literature, if he could help it.)

"But, it is true that a writer does express his own thoughts, through his characters. They—his characters—can express that part of the writer better than the writer can, himself. The characters become the writer's *id*. It's freeing.

"Many things, and all these play a part in his storytelling. To say that all is somehow autobiographical is to discredit the writer's imagination—his creative talent—which is found in every good storyteller. It's an insult, though few in the nonliterary world could ever recognize it as such."

"But, all I asked is, are you going to write about me?"

"No worries. If I do, I'll have it published under a pseudonym." Michael grinned, and Maud looked at him quizzically.

They sat for a quiet moment, while Maud stroked Susie's back. Finally, Michael continued: "I need this break from it all, for a while . . . maybe forever, I don't know, but long enough to think things through, to find myself again." Susie walked to Michael, and lay at his feet.

"I used to know other things—things besides teaching, besides literature—things that Frenchie had taught me," continued Michael. I used to see things in nature and wonder about them. The seasons had meaning for me—deep, inherent meaning. But, it's not that way now. I'm lost."

"That life doesn't exist anymore. It's gone forever. You've moved beyond all that, Michael. You're educated now."

"I know, I guess," said Michael, pensively, and then adding, "But, who am I? What do I belong to? You see, Maud, I thought I once knew. But, I don't anymore."

There was a long pause, but not necessarily an uncomfortable one, as Maud pondered Michael's questions. She'd always figured that Michael was Michael, a well-educated American man, originally from Crooked River. He was her son, and Frenchie's, too. That's who he was, and that's what he belonged to.

Finally, Maud broke the silence, "Stay as long as you'd like, Michael. *Mi casa es su casa*. My home is your home."

"Yeah, I know what it means. This *is* my home." But, Michael wasn't talking about the physical structure of Maud's house. It wasn't the home he'd ever lived in, those few short years in Crooked River. Maud's house could never be Michael's home. Only Crooked River was his home.

"Let me cook you breakfast now," said Maud, as she topped-off his cup of coffee, and then began unloading the refrigerator of eggs, bacon, veggies, salsa, sour cream, and just about anything else that could be used to make an omelet, and sourdough bread and butter.

"When you finish your cup, go ahead and get cleaned up, and I'll call you when breakfast is ready," she said, looking up from the refrigerator.

"Okay." He paused a moment, and then continued, "Um, do you have anything that might fit me, so I can wash my clothes?"

Maud walked into her bedroom and retrieved a woman's white terrycloth bathrobe.

"This is about all I have that might fit you, Honey," she said, chuckling, and Michael took it and walked into the guest bedroom. There he unloaded his travel bags of dirty clothes, some old manuscripts, and two books that he had saved: *To the Lighthouse*, and *A Portrait of the Artist as a Young Man*.

(Those were the first two adult novels Michael had read when he was a boy. He had always told himself that if he ever had a son, his son would inherit those books, among many others, thereby making it a tradition to pass on those stories. And, having a son would be different for Michael. For one, he wouldn't die. He'd be there for his son, to teach him and to protect him.)

Incredible! This is all of it, he thought, looking at what he had saved from his purge of the past. Everything he now owned fit in two travel bags, with some room to spare.

In the adjoining guest bathroom, Michael showered.

It was nighttime now. The air was cool and smelled like rain, so Michael and Maud, with Susie following close behind, left the patio and went back into the house. They sat at the kitchen table, with Susie again at Michael's feet.

"Would you like something to eat—some more roast beef, a piece of cake?"

"No, I'm still stuffed from supper." He hadn't eaten that well in a couple of weeks, and now his stomach was overreacting to it.

"I saw all those plaques and photos and whatnots on the wall of the guest room," said Michael. "You're quite the philanthropist."

"I do my best, Michael. I feel blessed that I can help out, and make other people's lives better, especially these poor Indians around here. Oh, I'm sorry; it's 'Native Americans' now, right?"

"'Indians' is fine—it's what the elders still say. Anyway, back to your philanthropy, is it all due to your inheritances and *shrewd* investments?"

"Yes, of course; I'm giving back to this community, for making me feel so welcomed and accepted."

"I've always figured you felt guilty for being one of the 'haves'. Do you feel guilt? That is to say, is it out of guilt for all that you have that makes you feel responsible for this community that has so very little?"

"You know, I *have* thought about that, but I think there are those who are born to be givers, and those that will always be takers. I'm one of the givers. And the Indians are the takers.

"I know you know I grew up around money, and I learned at a very early age that money begets money; that is, it takes money to make money. In every opportunity, every encounter, every person—except your father, of course—I looked at it as purely a way to make money. With your father, it was love.

"When I married your father, my parents chose to shun us. They didn't even acknowledge us, as a married couple. We were ostracized, even after you were born. They didn't want to see their new grandson. We were totally on our own, and couldn't count on them for anything. I'm sure it was to force me *to come to my senses* and divorce your father. But, I wouldn't. It was such a struggle, though: we had you; I quit teaching to take care of you and the household; and your father fished and trapped. It was all seasonal for him. When we needed help, Old Man LeBlanc was the only one who was there for us. That's how we survived, Michael. Somehow we survived.

"When I remarried, my parents were pleased with the choice I had made; my trust fund was reinstated, and so were my future bequeaths. I had only to wait patiently for their impending deaths.

"Our marriage was more like a corporate partnership, and I benefited greatly by it. That's why I have money. And that's why I can give it away.

"I'm a good person, Michael. Everyone in the community says so. Those plaques and such prove it. I don't feel guilty about any of that. I feel blessed."

Maud hesitated for a moment, and then changed the subject,   "There is something that I need to talk to you about. And, it's important." Maud paused to choose her words. "You're very thin. Your eyes are . . . well, they're dark and puffy." Maud paused again, but this time for an uncomfortable minute. "Honey, you're sick."

"I know. I need to quit smoking." Maud fidgeted.

"Don't get me wrong, I'm not judging you. But you look like your father's kin—you know, the ones up north," said Maud, when she found the courage to continue.

"The drunks?"

"Yes, Honey, the drunks." She paused, and again picked her words carefully: "I know these past few years have been very stressful on you: the car accident and losing your career." (She purposely excluded Helene, waiting for Michael to bring her up.)

"I didn't lose my career. I resigned," Michael answered, emphatically. Maud sat nervously silent. "It was too much for me," he added. "Right now, I need something less . . . a life less demanding, I guess. I need to produce, to create something that's my very own."

A break was what Michael needed most. Maybe China was it, where he might find what it was that he had once had. His writings had since evolved into something pedestrian, and he couldn't recognize them anymore: a perversion, a tangent from an approach that was now expressed indifferently, a lost and valuable thing.

Or, he wondered, was it reinvention, an evolution to a something new and not yet completed? Something that was still being developed? Had he outgrown his poetry, like so many poets before him, who then became novelists?

"Are you disappointed in me?" he asked.

"No, of course not." Maud hesitated, and then said, "Okay . . . well . . . I guess I am a little disappointed that you settled for something far below you. Michael, really, think about it: China? It's way below you."

"But, I like it there," said Michael.

"Losers teach in China."

"And, losers teach in America."

"But, not all of them are losers," answered Maud.

"Not every teacher in China is a loser! People are there for many different reasons, not just that they can't find work in their own countries." Maud looked at him disbelievingly, as if saying, 'Only a crazy person would choose to live in China over America.'

But, to give some credence to Maud's broad generalizations, it was true in that the few so-called losers in China that Michael had actually met were loud, obnoxious, socially inept Americans, with tendencies toward threats and bouts of rage and, of course, substance abuse. Their public behaviors gave the impression that all Americans in China were losers, so much so that Michael, when asked by Chinese people on the street, "Hello, where are you from?" quickly replied "*Fa guo*" (France). It was less bothersome that way. It killed the conversation immediately at that answer, in that few Chinese could speak French.

"Really, I've worked with some very talented educators from all over the world. They're well-educated and knowledgeable in their areas of expertise. Many of them have doctorates, particularly the Europeans—the Germans and the French, especially—and many of the Japanese have doctorates, as well," said Michael.

"Japanese, what are they doing in China? I thought China and Japan hated each other."

"Well, they do most of the time, but China needs teachers of all languages," answered Michael.

"Well, everybody knows that Europeans and Asians aren't educated like Americans. We're better than they are."

"Maud!"

"Since Americans think everybody in China is a loser, then that's all that counts," said Maud, adding, "Why don't you find yourself a job at Wal-Mart, a temporary job 'til something else . . . a better job comes along? Maybe the night-shift, so no one would see you. Or an office job. They make more money than you do in China."

"So do drug dealers. I'm educated. You said so yourself."

"Then go back to the university. Use your education, and be paid for it," replied Maud.

"First of all, I don't want to go back. And secondly, I really doubt they'd take me back."

"What about Loch, maybe he can help."

"It's over. I'm sorry that you're embarrassed, that your prominent professor son is now a so-called loser. But, I don't care what Americans think, and I never will. You've *got* to get over it."

"But Michael, you worked so hard. All those awards! At a university, a real university, an *American* university, is where you belong," answered Maud.

To Maud, Michael's departure from American academia, and then teaching in China, endangered her good reputation in the community. All that she had done for Michael created this Crooked River's success story: "Michael is a nationally renowned academic and writer." Now, it appeared to her, but mostly to the community, that she had erred in her choices for Michael. Maud feared criticism and chastisement. Deep inside, she wanted to admit that she was wrong, but she couldn't. To the community, Maud didn't make mistakes; she was never wrong. She was blessed, after all.

"Listen, most of what I did, I did for Helene," answered Michael. Helene loved the life they had created in their small city on the Rocky Mountain Front. Michael could have seen himself staying there until retirement, but only for her. Michael continued: "But, Helene is gone."

"Honey," said Maud, "Helene didn't go, didn't leave, didn't abandon you. It wasn't planned. It wasn't malicious, done in spite, purposeful, or anything like that. She loved you, dearly. It was the brain aneurism, Michael. You've got to face the fact that she's dead. She's not coming back."

Michael sat still, staring straight ahead at nothing. It was as if he needed reaffirmation, to hear it once again, the reason Helene was missing from his life. And, so, he quietly concurred, "I know. I know." His eyes became teary.

Maud put her arms around Michael, and hugged him tightly.

"It's hard," he choked, when he could finally utter a few words. "I'm not me without her. And, I'm not sure if I can do this . . . I mean, go on without her. She was perfect."

Helene's death kept Michael confined in that one last moment of freedom before she died, like a coyote stepping into a trap, attempting to run away from it, the drag hooking on a root. Exhausted from the struggle to break free, Michael waited for the inevitable end, unable to escape that final moment, when the jaws unexpectedly snapped shut. The clock had stopped.

"I know that's what you remember now, but Helene wasn't perfect. No one is. And, you had a wonderful marriage, but it wasn't perfect either," said Maud.

Again, Michael stared wide-eyed, straight ahead at nothing.

Maud continued, "You'll always remember Helene—all the good times, and not the bad ones, certainly not her death and funeral—and you'll miss her, of course. That's what matters most: those fond memories that you two created together."

"I still talk to her all the time."

"It's normal for right now, I think," said Maud.

"I don't think you understand me. She comes to me. She's actually right there with me, and we talk," said Michael.

"Oh, dear." Maud sat silent for a minute, and then said, "Honey, listen to me, it's time now. Mourn Helene, and when you see her again, if you see her again, tell her goodbye. Then, you'll be able to go on and become alive again, and write those wonderful poems."

"What was it like when Frenchie died? Did you feel that you couldn't go on?"

"Yes. I never thought I could live without him. Did you know we fought the day he left? I've always regretted that."

Michael tried to remember the morning of the day Helene died, when they had had their morning coffee, before they started their workday. What had they talked about? Had he told her he loved her, as he walked out the door? Or had they argued?

"You fought about me, didn't you?" Michael asked.

"Does it really matter? The thing is I mourned your father; I forgave him for dying—Michael, forgiveness is a powerful thing, don't ever forget that—and I found the strength to get my life back. It took a little while for me to accept his death, but not as long as you might imagine. And, that's what will happen to you."

"Okay, I'll try."

Michael stayed up all night.

It was a Tuesday that day, and Michael and Helene had just returned from French Polynesia, the weekend before last. It happened so suddenly. It was so surreal:

Michael was in his office, reviewing lecture notes, when Loch busted through the door.

"Michael, it's Helene. You must get to the hospital at once. I'll drive." He was huffing and puffing, and sweating profusely; his eyes were wild with fright.

At the hospital, Becky was there to meet him, and then everyone was there. Everyone, but whom?—he couldn't remember any of them now, just people, standing around, sitting quietly; only empty faces . . .

She—Becky—told him that they'd been at a coffee shop, planning their next trip to who-knows-where, when all of a sudden Helene let out a loud groan, and dropped her head to the table.

There was a funeral, of course. He didn't remember much: Maud was there, sitting next to him, and he did remember the coffin being shut . . . that's about it, the coffin being shut. His doctor must have given him something—Valium, most likely—and a month later it was as if he had finally woken, while lecturing on William Carlos Williams:

". . . I feel that I would like/to go there/and fall into those flowers/and sink into the marsh near them."

How had he done it? How had Michael taught all those classes?

Maud awoke at about 2 A.M. to find Michael sitting at the kitchen table, his eyes red and swollen, and his arms wrapped around himself, rocking back and forth, saying goodbye to Helene.

"Venice", "kittens", "the accordion player" were all audible in his soft mumblings, and Maud knew he was reciting the story of his marriage proposal to Helene.

Michael didn't see Maud standing there—she, herself, now crying—and she left him alone, and quietly returned to bed.

"I'm so sorry you died, Helene. I'd do anything to have you back. But, I know I can't."

Michael forgave Helene for dying, and himself for blaming her for dying, telling her that he loved her so deeply, he would always love her, and he would never forget her. With Helene, Michael had been the happiest ever. But—

"Helene, my sweet girl, it's time for me to let you go. I have to. I'm trying to get my life back. I know that would be what you'd want.

"I'm but scattered shards of what I was with you."

And, then sitting at the table across from Michael was Helene.

"Are you okay, Michael?"

"No, of course not, I'm trying to say goodbye to you."

"I know. And I agree, Michael, you must go on."

"It's going to be difficult, isn't it?" he asked.

"It's going to be possible."

"Do you know that I woke up one morning, not so very long ago, feeling so good, so happy? I rolled over to look at your lovely face—you were so beautiful, when you were sleeping—like I used to do. Did you know that I used to do that? But, you weren't there. You were gone. I must have been dreaming about you. And, then I remembered . . . then, it all came back to me. Oh, Helene!—I don't know if I can do this," he gasped and choked.

"You can, and you will. But it's going to be a difficult, necessary journey. You're already on the first leg, and at the end you'll find yourself again. Then you'll be able to go on. I'm going to be there, Michael. You can't get rid of me simply by saying goodbye."

At daybreak, Michael scribbled a shaky note, letting Maud know that he had gone out to the 4-O-5 (pronounced "four-oh-five")—he felt he needed to be close to Frenchie—and that he wouldn't be back until dark.

One evening after supper, and after "Wheel" and "Jeopardy" (Maud was a whiz at "Jeopardy")—

Alex: This Nineteenth Century Cherokee man developed an alphabet, called a syllabary, for his nation.

Maud: "Who was Sequoya?"

—Maud asked, "Will you take a lover in China? Sex *is* very healthy, Michael."

"I know, and I would like to find someone to do things with, like travel, try new restaurants, coffee shops, go to the cinema, and so on. But, I don't know how easy or difficult it's going to be. It seems to me that Chinese people, especially the women, are quite suspicious of foreigners. And, I'm not sure why."

"I hope you can find someone who will take care of you. You were so handsome, when you were with Helene. She took good care of you, Honey."

"I know. So, . . . like, what . . . I'm ugly now?" he asked, grinning.

"No, of course not, just a bit disheveled."

"Okay, I'll try to become *sheveled* in China."

"Sheveled is not a word," said Maud.

"I know; I make my living with words. I was trying to be funny."

"Oh yes, I remember your sense of humor. You were such a strange boy," she replied.

For the remainder of the evening, the conversation-killer (TV) reigned, and at about 10 P.M. Maud decided to retire for the evening. As she was about say good night to Michael, he asked, "Why did Frenchie call me his 'little *goret*'?"

Maud thought about it for a moment and then said, "That means 'piglet', Michael."

"Yeah, I know what it means. I just don't know why he called me that."

"It's from a story: a little pig on an adventure to find . . . soup. I think it was a metaphor. Anyway, he told it to you many, many times, when you were small. It was your favorite, and I think it was your father's favorite too," said Maud.

"Yeah, I remember it a little . . . something about a bear, and there were chickens, a scary, rickety bridge. Oh, and coyote was there too, right?"

"I'm not sure, anymore. But you know, at one time, I wrote down some of his stories for posterity. I have to say, your father threw such a fit about it. He even called me an ethnologist."

They laughed.

Maud continued, "So, I had to listen to them over and over again, and then quickly scribble some notes in a notebook, so that you'd have them when you were grown. I wonder where that notebook is now."

"I sure would like to read it," said Michael.

"It would be in that notebook—the pig story, that is—I'm sure of it. Let me think about where it could be."

Maud was certain it was somewhere in the house. It had to be. She never threw anything out. But, maybe someone had borrowed it. She thought she could remember someone borrowing it.

LI QIN

IN MICHAEL'S SECOND SEMESTER at Heilongjiang Foreign Studies Institute, the inevitable happened.

After class, Michael was climbing the stairs to his office. Upon hearing his name being called, he turned to see a tall, sleek, attractive girl—an oblong, white face, with round eyes, her hair in a bun with bangs, dressed in tight, straight-leg blue jeans, high heels, and a loose-fitting Winnie the Pooh sweatshirt; in other words, the epitome of a *Dongbei* (northeast) girl—hurrying to catch up with him. There was something vaguely familiar about her, but his classes were large, upwards of 120 students in his literature class. So, getting to know individual students was a difficult, if not impossible, task.

"Michael," she began, out of breath, "may I talk to you?"

"Sure, I'm heading to my office right now. Walk with me."

"I would like to meet with you," she panted.

"Why?"

"To practice my English, of course," still catching her breath. Michael stopped on a landing, for her sake.

"Well, my office hours are usually after sixth hour."

"Okay, then I'll begin tomorrow," she insisted. Her eyes smiled, and she turned to leave.

"Wait! What's your name?"

"Li Qin. My foreign name is Eleanor, but you may call me Li Qin," she said. "Don't you remember me? I talked to you last semester . . . by the fountain? We talked about T.S. Eliot's poem, "The Love Song of J. Alfred Prufrock"? I'm working on my master's degree in English?"

"Sorry, too many students," said Michael, slowly shaking his head back and forth.

"That's okay. I left my hair long and straight last semester. What do you think about it now?"

Michael, still overtly Americanized, in that he was excessively cautious of sexual harassment allegations (an unreality in China), thought it best not to answer Li Qin. He only smiled (and bit his lower lip), and Li Qin giggled, turned, and skipped her way back down the stairs.

The next day they began meeting in his office, a converted small classroom, on the top floor. But, Michael shared his office with four colleagues, and the atmosphere at times was loud and disruptive. A month later they changed the meeting place to Michael's apartment. It was quieter there and less inhibited, they both agreed.

Soon, they began spending time together on weekends, reading, listening to music, watching movies, and talking. Michael told Li Qin about his travels to places like Paris and Madrid (one summer, when Michael and Helene were graduate students, they toured the places found in *The Sun Also Rises*, Michael's favorite Hemingway novel), and the many places he had lived. He told her about the books he had read and loved and his fascination with early Modernism. He told her about the people he had met and known along the way, and the ones he most admired. Some of what he had told Li Qin was (to be frank) posturing. But, she listened and dreamed, her dark, far-away eyes shining. Michael's apartment became a refuge for her, with a peacefulness she couldn't find on campus or anywhere else.

One day Michael called Li Qin to ask if she wanted to go out for coffee. He had heard about a new coffee shop in the city, *Douceur de Vivre*, and wanted to try it.

Li Qin asked, "Would it be Dutch?"

"I'm thinking more like French roast," answered Michael. There was a moment of silence.

"No, what I meant was—"

"If I invite you, then it's my treat," said Michael, smiling into the phone.

"But, our dear professor of American culture told us that if a man pays, then it's considered a date."

"Is your professor Chinese?"

"But of course."

"Well, it's not necessarily a date. But, if this is something you're uncomfortable with, you could invite a friend to join us. It really doesn't matter to me."

For Li Qin, it was more of a matter of being seen in public with a foreigner, especially a middle-aged one. Michael was older, and to Chinese people westerners looked much older than their age. It was frowned upon, and she knew she'd get "the look of scorn" from elder women. Would they think that she was a prostitute? But, she wanted to accompany Michael. She knew and trusted him by then.

"Let's make a plan," Li Qin said.

"Okay, but why do we need a plan?"

"We can't be seen together. People will talk," replied Li Qin.

"Okay, then why don't you go to the coffee shop first, and then I'll arrive a few minutes later and join you there. Should I wear a disguise—maybe a thick mustache, a sombrero, and a multicolored poncho?"

"If you wish."

"I was joking, Li Qin."

"Oh, I don't understand the joke."

"*Machs nichts.*"

"Huh?"

"It doesn't matter."

So, Li Qin arrived at *Douceur de Vivre* at 2 P.M., Michael at 2:10 P.M., and they spent the afternoon in the coffee shop, talking, listening to eclectic, international music, and watching each other's every gesture and expression. Afterward, as they stood up to leave the coffee shop, Li Qin looked around, making sure no one was watching, wrapped her arm around Michael's, stood tippy-toed, and gave him a quick peck on the cheek.

"That was nice," Michael said; and a surprise, he thought.

"I really enjoy being with you, Michael." Her eyes sparkled, and she couldn't stop smiling.

A Sunday soon after, Li Qin came over to Michael's to watch *Roman Holiday*, a favorite among his students.

Afterward, Michael made fajitas for them, and they shared a bottle of wine. (Michael's alcohol consumption had decreased to an occasional glass of red wine at that time. He felt settled in his new life in China, and Li Qin's attention helped matters, too.) Li Qin was getting a little tipsy, and being forward with the use of sexual innuendo. But, Michael resisted, much to Li Qin's disappointment. Out of frustration, Li Qin finally asked, "Aren't you going to have sex with me? "

"No."

"Why, what's wrong with me?" she whined.

"Absolutely nothing's wrong with you, but you're kind of drunk right now. I want you to be sober, when we make love for the first time," answered Michael. Drunken sex would only have reminded him of Geri, whom he chose to forget.

"Can I at least have a kiss?"

"Okay, you can have a kiss," answered Michael, and then added, "But it's got to stop there, okay?"

"Okay."

So, Michael kissed Li Qin, a long, deep, passionate kiss. And, the affair began later in the week.

But, for Li Qin, the affair had become difficult from the start. There was the threat of being exposed and, if so, shame would ensue. Michael could be fired. She spoke to Michael about it, but he hadn't any answers. For him, being quite self-centered, and not fully understanding Chinese culture (a maligning ignorance at the time), figured it was a nonissue. To him, losing a teaching job in China was like having his cell phone stolen on a city bus. It would be initially aggravating; there'd be a one-time monetary setback to replace it; and, within a day, he'd have another one. Then, he could continue on with his life, as before.)

But, Li Qin was guilt-ridden and confused.

Li Qin came from a broken home, from poor, uneducated, working-class parents: her mother a saleswoman (called "seller", in the vernacular), and her father a security guard at a gated apartment complex. Being poor (possibly too poor to adequately bribe an official), the only way for their daughter to do well in life—and therefore in theirs—was to marry into a good family, a step above hers. Beauty would go far, would attract many suitors, but certainly not far enough to land her a wealthy Chinese groom.

Wanting out of China, free from a tyrannical Chinese mother, the burden of being born female, and a poverty she would know her entire life, Li Qin had a plan. She wanted to see the world, to experience people and places, like Michael had so often described, to live free in the West.

Li Qin cared little for filial piety, of marrying a Chinese boy, of becoming a mother and a Chinese wife. Experiencing first hand her parents' split-up, she didn't want to marry into an arrangement; she didn't want to become her mother. The life Li Qin would have in China, she foresaw, would be nothing more than that of a tethered sheep. After all, that was her mother's life. But, Michael (any westerner for that matter) could offer her the means to break away from such a burden. She could have the life of young American women, so convincing in Hollywood movies, unfettered, free from feigned Chinese morality, her body manipulated, utilized, exploited, plundered by lovers. She would have many lovers.

So, early on, she began using the term "love" with Michael: "I'm such a lucky girl, to have such a beautiful man as you, Michael. I love you." But, she knew nothing of love, only its definition in her Chinese-English/English-Chinese Collegiate Dictionary, which she had memorized and could recite at a moment's notice. Love was an abstraction, a mere four-letter word to Li Qin. She had nothing else to compare it to.

Indecisive, apprehensive, excited, terrified, embarrassed, pleased, thrown, her emotions ran the gamut, with two worlds pulling at her; Li Qin didn't know what to do.

At a nondescript noodle restaurant in the city center, Li Qin and her mother were having lunch. Li Qin seemed different, quieter to her mother, so the mother asked, "Is there something wrong?"

"No, mother, I'm tired, that's all."

"Aren't you getting enough rest?"

"Yes, of course; I'm just tired today."

Her mother wasn't convinced.

The conversation soon turned from gentle, maternal attentiveness to an interrogation, and Li Qin finally confessed: "I have a boyfriend, and he's an American teacher, who's older than I am." It was liberating for Li Qin to finally come clean; the mother, however, saw it differently.

"What?! You are a stupid, naïve girl," Li Qin's mother told her. "He is a devil! Do you want to go to America just to become a prostitute, is that what you want?—because that's what you'll be. The devil thinks nothing of you—no! He thinks only of himself."

But, Li Qin knew that her mother would use any tactic to save face. The affair would be shameful, an embarrassment for Li Qin to be seen with an older American lover. The mother contrived scenarios of how her family, their neighbors, and her former teachers would be publicly ridiculed. And, the list went on and on. There'd be no end to the embarrassment.

"You must end this crazy affair immediately," her mother told her. "You are giving me a terrible headache."

So, later that day, Li Qin ended the affair with a brief text message: "It's over. I'm Sorry." It was partly out of concern for her mother's health, but mostly out of guilt.

But, a few days later, Li Qin returned to Michael.

She asked, "What it is, Michael? Why can't I stay away from you?"

"You've told me many times that you've given me your heart," he said confidently, and then added, "You've said that there's only room for *me* in there."

(Li Qin regularly spoke in Chinese proverbs, idioms, clichés, and pop song lyrics, which generally lacked originality. It could also be construed as lacking sincerity. It was common among the more traditional Chinese groups, in that their education stressed rote learning—critical and creative thinking were nonexistent— especially the memorization of inspirational words of wisdom.

But there was something else at play. Giving your heart and giving your body were two separate things. Li Qin could easily convince Michael that he had her heart, while at the same time giving her body to others. The former was love; the latter was desire or duty. It was culturally acceptable among many traditional members. Michael was, however, oblivious to it at that time. He took everything at face value, within his cultural constructs.)

Li Qin thought about their affair often, probably far too often, and her plan to leave China. It would still take some time, she knew. There was her mother to contend with, and she (the mother) had the power of veto.

"It will be Michael, or it will be another foreigner. Either way, it will be one more year before I will finish my master's, and then I can leave. It will all be worth it," she told herself continuously, thinking in that Chinese-Machiavellian kind of way.

Patiently, she waited.

Over the next six months, Michael and Li Qin's affair settled into a comfortable, though somewhat unexciting, routine. Love for them was temporal and spatial. In public, they were acquaintances. Often, he'd run into Li Qin and her sisters (she called her roommates "sisters")—Su Wan Rong, Wang Qi (the pretty one), and Chen Hao—strolling along the streets in the city center, window-shopping. But, in Michael's apartment, on Li Qin's biweekly visits, they were lovers. Michael was happy with the arrangement: Li Qin made him feel appreciated and desired, but mostly like the young grad student that he once was. She was his mirror. And, she reminded him of Helene, when he and Helene were first dating. He saw Helene in her every movement, in her every expression.

For Michael, sex was a natural expression of love. It was his responsibility to bring her the utmost pleasure. He was a tender lover.

It would be better with Li Qin; *he* would be better, he told himself. He was more attentive, more considerate and responsive, having learned his lesson too late with Helene.

But, for Li Qin, it was different. The constant conflict inside her persisted. She knew she could easily manipulate Michael using sex; he was desperate for love. Sex made love real, made it all true, and Michael couldn't separate the two.

She could take him, possess him, deceive him (any foreigner could serve her purpose, but Michael seemed to be an easy target for her; all she needed to do was to tell him that she loved him), and yet she could remain free. Sex held no attachment for her.

"It is sexy time now," she would mechanically say, while disrobing, tossing her clothes upon the foot of the bed, and walking to the shower. Sex was simply a means to keep him there, to keep him interested in her. And, she focused on the trophy: a life outside of China.

But, her mother remained unyielding and oppressive.

One day, Li Qin came to Michael's apartment visibly upset.

"My mother said that American teachers are fakes. She said that they can't find work in America. They make false documents, so they can teach in China," which was a commonly held belief among Chinese people (and many foreigners, as well).

"Some do," Michael replied, adding, "But most of those are BIA people, and other teachers at private language schools."

"B . . . A?"

"BIA: a British private language school in China. These types of schools hire young, uneducated people: 'dancing, white monkeys', we call them. But, there are other ridiculous names, too."

"Monkeys?!"

"Yes, well, sort of . . . but not actually 'monkeys', per se. You see, the teachers are there to entertain the students, to sing and dance, to make them laugh. If they're liked, the students will stay with the program, and the school will continue to make money. Usually the teachers are male and handsome, at least to Chinese people. Since the students' mothers are footing the bill, they're happy too. They have something to look at and maybe sleep with. Everybody wins: the school, the kids, the mothers, the 'dancing, white monkeys'

"BIA is more like a McDonald's Playland than a language school. It's kind of like how the Churchies—

"Churchies?"

"Yeah, you know, those teachers at the institute that are part of that Christian organization. They teach first year students."

"Oh, okay. I've never heard them called 'Churchies' before."

"Anyway, the Churchies really don't do much teaching. They're afraid to correct the students' English—pronunciation, collocation, whatever—for fear of alienating them, or themselves from the students. They only want to be liked. They feel that they can attract more flies with honey than vinegar. So, what they do is entertain their students. And, rarely do they give final scores below ninety percent. Their students are happy little morons, who are totally misled."

"Oh, I got a ninety percent in my first-year oral English class." Li Qin paused to contemplate what Michael had just told her. He tried hard not to smile.

"How was your second year—harder?" Michael asked. Li Qin nodded. "Of course, it was," he added, "you were taught by a real teacher.

"Anyway," Michael continued, "there's at least one BIA in the city, maybe more. They're all over China, but, really, who cares?

"Li Qin, you need to understand something: here, at Heilongjiang Foreign Studies Institute, most of the foreign teachers are well educated. Churchies aside, more than half of the teachers have at least a master's and some have doctorates. And, most have prior university teaching experience," he explained.

"In fact, the older teachers are normally retired professors from their own countries. There was a retired American professor here from Rutgers University. It's a good school. People come here for many different reasons. A young guy from America, who attended Columbia University for his master's, was here to take a break, before going on for his doctorate. A French couple, retired from the Diplomatic Corps, only wanted to live in China for a year, just to travel and experience the different cultures here. Many teachers are writers and poets. I met a filmmaker, who was making a documentary. Many are here to learn Chinese. One was here to learn *real* Tai Chi. (Michael purposely left out the teachers that he suspected were actually human rights activists.) You should tell your mother all this," Michael added.

Li Qin replied, "No, I won't, Michael. My mother is very ill. It's her legs this time. She can't walk without a cane now. We must never see each other again." And, with that, Li Qin stomped out the door.

Michael took a walk outside campus, and then back to his office. Serge, a French scholar, was sitting at a computer playing solitaire. A generation senior to Michael, Serge was short, quite thin and bald, with a scruffy white goatee. He wore pants too short, and his shirts and blazers were spotted with numerous stains of various sizes; in all his years in China, Serge had yet to master chopsticks. His clothes smelled of stale cigarette smoke, and his index and middle fingers on his left hand were stained yellow, as were his teeth. His handshake was flaccid.

Embodying latent French Imperialism, Serge married, and soon thereafter divorced, four foreign women, all of whom were from developing nations in Asia and Africa, which he *ironically* called the "excitable, hairless races". All four were mothers to his four sons. None of the wives were from China, yet. Serge was actively searching for a new wife. It had been a couple of years since his latest divorce, and there was still time left for Serge. He was ageless.

And, true to French spirit, Serge was emotionally charged and inappropriately loud. In other words, he epitomized the French man of his generation.

For those very reasons, of all the expats that Michael had met in China, he enjoyed Serge's company most.

Michael and Serge had first communicated, beyond cordial greetings, the semester prior in Dining Hall #3

"You were in Nigeria?"

"Yes, Lagos, for six years," said Serge.

"Doing what?"

"I was an economist with the World Bank."

"Wow!—sounds interesting." Michael was impressed.

"Yes. But Lagos, it is a special place. Do you know, my Dear, that in Lagos, it is the first time I ate human flesh (meaning "human meat")?"

"Ate . . . What?! Human flesh?"

"Yes, you see in Lagos at that time, when a person was killed in a traffic accident, his body went either to the morgue or to restaurants."

"No, you're joking."

"I am afraid not. It is all true. There was a shortage of flesh. In fact, the national zoo, it was without animals. All had been eaten!"

"*Bonjour*, Serge."

"*Bonjour*, Michel. Why are you grinning so?"

"I just heard a funny joke out by the front gate. Want to hear it?"

"Yes, by all means," answered Serge.

"Okay, as I passed the taxis at the gate, one driver called out to me, 'ha-row (hello)'. The other drivers were all in stitches."

"Yes, the gauntlet, it is a problem," said Serge, without emotion. After a short pause, Serge remembered a question he'd wanted to ask Michael, or any American for that matter. "Michel, I do need an American oxymoron. Please, Dear, do you have one I can use?"

"Professional geographer," quipped Michael.

"Very nice, very nice, oh, ho, ho," Serge chuckled. "But, in France, geographers are respected professionals. Many are military strategists."

"A French military strategist? Hmm, you know something, I think *that's* an oxymoron," said Michael, and Serge looked seriously confused.

"Now *I* have a question for you. It's kind of personal," said Michael.

"Ask away, although I may not answer it truthfully."

"You've been in China a long time, right?"

"Twelve years, but that is not a very personal question."

"There's more—have you ever dated a Chinese woman?"

"But of course. In fact, I am dating one now. No, no, that is not true. I am dating *two* now: a woman *and* a girl. The girl, she's quite beautiful, I must say; the woman not so much, but she's appreciative of my attention. And, she can cook." Michael grinned.

"I'm wondering about tradition—Chinese tradition. I can't seem to figure it out," said Michael.

"Well, Michel, with tradition, it is a losing game in matters of romance, I am sorry to say. If I might make a suggestion, try to find a doctor or a professor. She has been busy with her studies well past marrying age. It's normally 30, or younger in some cases, as you may well know. A well-educated woman is less influenced by tradition."

Michael nodded in agreement, not that he knew Serge was right, but that it made sense to him.

Serge continued, "You might not know this, my dear, but with a traditional Chinese girl—you do know that a woman is called a girl before she's married, regardless of age—if you decide to marry her, it is imperative that you become responsible for her family. It is very likely that her parents would take possession of your—how do you say . . . oh, yes!—remuneration, and make available to you only a small, monthly allowance. It is a trap!"

Michael was taken aback. *What?!—shouldn't somebody have told me this before now?*

"There's more. A man's age is a complicated issue, as well. You've might have heard: 'It is better to be an old man's darling, than a young man's slave.' This is not necessarily true with a traditional Chinese girl. She is made to believe that it is honorable to be her husband's slave. But, an older, professional woman would be delighted to be an old man's darling."

"Could that also mean that she's desperate?"

"Yes, and that is usually the case. My suggestion, Michel, is to have fun with the girls, but be serious about the women."

Michael picked up a book from his desk and started out the door.

Serge called out, "Michel, whatever happened to that beautiful girl you were tutoring in here?"

"She lost interest."

"I see. But, I am not convinced. This is the land of deception. Young Chinese girls are not interested in practicing their English—no, no. They are only interested in being around a handsome boy . . . or in your case a handsome man."

"Thanks," said Michael, "for the information and the compliment."

"Don't mention it," answered Serge, with a nod, as he turned back to the computer to finish his game.

The pattern was predictable and Michael knew it well:

First, either Li Qin or her mother would mention Michael's name to the other (this, he could only presume);

Next, Li Qin's mother would allege something dishonorable about Michael's character or culture, adding that the affair was causing her health to deteriorate;

Then, Li Qin, convinced of the allegation and concerned for her mother, would end their relationship;

And finally, in less than a week, Li Qin would ask Michael to take her back.

A few days later Li Qin showed up at Michael's door, and they were back to their routine of one midweek (usually Wednesday) and Sunday conjugal visits, as Michael aptly called them.

For the next few months, Li Qin, like a Libra in a pet store, bouncing back and forth between two bird cages—one silver and the other gold—in an attempt to choose the best one to purchase, kept the "on-again", of their on-again-off-again affair within the walls of Michael's apartment. She began to call his apartment "home", and they joked about their comfortable married life together. For him, it was natural and predictable: a simple reality, a continuation of what he had had with Helene. There weren't those "Isaac Davis" insecurities in their relationship. Everything to him was quite genuine, until the next "off-again", which was expected. Still, he found it less frustrating than entertaining.

For Li Qin, the affair was simply killing time.

THE BETRAYAL

A CONDUCTOR STEPPED into the car and announced the next station, which startled Michael back to the crowded, noisy car, and the old man with the cigarettes sitting across from him.

When he had finished speaking, the conductor left the car, and Michael turned to the old man, smiled, and said, "Five years ago, I can't believe it—this adventure of mine—began five years ago."

The old man looked puzzled.

"Five years," said Michael, while gesturing the number five with his hand. "It was five years ago that Helene died." Michael paused momentarily, sighed, but then quickly continued, "Six months later I was in Ukraine, on a Fulbright. Then, I was in a near-fatal car accident in Canada. I resigned from my professorship. I worked—if you can call it that—on a small ranch. I came to China to teach. I fell in love, again. I fell out of love. I slept with an incredibly beautiful, intelligent woman. Amazing, don't you think? I mean, so what's next? Just think about it: the places I've been, and the people I've met all along the way. Wouldn't you say it's been an unbelievable five-year journey—even *with* the heartaches?"

The old man grinned, as if he understood Michael. It was as if they had somehow connected, and Michael thought, wow!—this is too cool. But then—

"Oh, no thank you. I'm serious. Really, I couldn't smoke another cigarette, even if I wanted to. But, thanks anyway," said Michael.

The trained slowed and then stopped in Siping, and the generous old man with the cigarettes nodded goodbye and disembarked. In his place came a young woman, carrying an infant and leading a toddler. The toddler sat between his mother's legs, while she cradled the infant in her arms the entire way to Harbin. And, a young couple came—a foreign man, whose nationality wasn't obvious, with a Chinese woman—and sat kitty-corner across the aisle from Michael. He made no effort to talk to either of them, and they glanced only once in his direction. Michael thought about describing them in his field notes, but he had grown sleepy by then. And, both seemed to him to be bored with life, or with each other. Departing a few minutes later, the train continued into the countryside.

There were scattered villages of farm families, and, as the train passed one, Michael saw a group of magpies on the ground and in a clump of trees near the tracks. He thought about a poem by an American poet living in China, in the late 1970s or early 80s. It was in an obscure poetry journal, but he couldn't remember the poet's name or even the publication now. Too many years had passed. Michael had once used the poem to demonstrate explication to his students, when he was a young (enthusiastic) and promising assistant professor.

The title of the poem was "On the Commons" (or, maybe it was the singular "Common", Michael wasn't sure, anymore), and he recited it out loud, but only to the window:

Thirteen magpies chase their shadows,
Remains of summer, fast departing,
Familiar now, a thing too casual?
When magpies join in groups to winter.

As he explained the use of numerology, symbols, word usage, and very likely allusions to his students, Michael reasoned that the poem was about a summer love affair between an American man and a Chinese woman (rarely was it the other way around). The affair had become unexciting and far too predictable, so it ended in the fall. By diagramming the entire poem, line by line and word by word on the blackboard, Michael deduced that the park-like setting in the poem was a simple metaphor, and not necessarily a physical description. Michael was quite sure he'd hit the mark. His students were amazed at his insight. They actually hooted and applauded, when he finished.

Turning back from the window, Michael closed his eyes and tried to sleep. But, an evening in late April came to mind. Michael had been Li Qin's only lover at the time. They had made love, and then parted for the night—

"Beautiful, isn't it?" It was a clear, deep blue evening in Harbin. Soft glowing, yellow bulbs lined each walkway on campus; a full moon upon the pond: the view from Michael's sixth-floor apartment.

Li Qin's answer was only a sigh. She hugged Michael tightly, and kissed his back softly.

"I'm going to be late," she said matter-of-factly, dropping her towel, and picking through the pile of clothes at the foot of the bed. Michael watched her dress in the soft moonlight.

"You should stay the night," he offered, but then laughed.

"If you want me to, I will," she said, sincerely.

"No. It'd be too risky. I was only joking. I thought you'd find it funny."

"I love you, Baby," she whispered, then kissed him quickly and left the apartment.

Then, Michael finally fell asleep to the rhythm of the train.

One Friday in early May, Michael left campus for the city: his biweekly shopping trip, for French roast coffee and block sharp cheddar cheese, at a small Western store in the city center. Afterward, he stopped by McDonald's, as was his routine.

At a small table for two near a window, as he sat down (but before he began eating his Big Mac meal), Michael checked his phone for messages. There weren't any, so he set the phone on the table and began to eat. When finished, he left McDonald's for home, forgetting the phone where he had laid it.

Moments later, Brad, a young American teacher, walked to the same table—it was the only open table; it had yet to be cleared and cleaned—and brushed aside some containers, wrappers, and napkins, thereby discovering Michael's phone. He opened it, and found multiple messages to and from Li Qin. Searching the photos, he found a series of nudes—tastefully done, though thoroughly revealing—of her.

About that same time Li Qin left campus alone to buy a new bag in the city. Her old bag was far too childish. It was pink vinyl, with the logo of a Disney character on it (one of the many princesses), but she wanted to project a more sophisticated image. After all, within a month, she would graduate with a Master of Arts degree in English.

On the bus, Li Qin received a phone call from Michael's number.

"Hi, Michael," answered Li Qin.

"Ah, yeah, well, this isn't Michael. I found this phone at McDonald's. It had your number in it."

"Oh, um . . . it belongs to a friend of mine: Michael."

"Can we meet somewhere? I'd like to give it back."

"Sure. I'm on my way into the city right now. How about at *Douceur de Vivre*, in about an hour?"

"That's a coffee shop on Jilin Street, right?"

"Yes, that's it."

At the coffee shop, Li Qin lost herself in Brad's stories of travel and adventure, and in his eyes—they actually changed color with changes in the light. She thought he was the most handsome boy she had ever met, and wondered if he could be "The One".

Li Qin asked, "So where do you teach?"

"At BIA—ever heard of it?"

"It's a private school, right?" Li Qin giggled, remembering what Michael had said about BIA. And, he was right, she thought. 'Brad is so handsome!'

"Yeah, the school's not far from here. Want to see it?"

"Sure."

They finished their coffee, and Brad led Li Qin by the hand to the school. She felt an electrical current in his touch, like nothing she'd ever felt before.

"That's it," said Brad, pointing to the school. "There's really not much to see: identical classrooms on three floors."

They stood through an awkward moment of silence, and then Brad added, "And that's my apartment—that window right up there." He put his head next to hers and pointed, so she could follow his finger to the window.

Li Qin laughed and asked, "Your apartment has only one window?"

"On his side, yeah, but there's another one on the other side."

They both chuckled, and then Brad asked, "Do you want to see my apartment?"

"Why not?" answered Li Qin.

In Brad's apartment:

Li Qin glanced coyly over to Brad; he pulled her to him, and they kissed. Li Qin pulled away; Brad pursued. He pushed Li Qin back against the wall; they kissed again. Li Qin pushed him away; their eyes met.

A moment passed.

With her eyes still fixated on Brad's, Li Qin pulled her T-shirt up and over her head; Brad undid her jeans and, slipping his hands in at her hips, slid them and her panties down to her knees. Li Qin took his hand, and guided it to her pussy.

"Ooh, yes," she murmured through a heavy breath, draped her arms over his shoulders, and rested her forehead against his chin.

Naked and sitting cross-legged on the bed, Brad and Li Qin faced each other. He lit a bowl and offered it to her, but she declined.

"I'll be back," said Li Qin, as she got up and walked to the bathroom.

When she returned and climbed back onto the bed, Brad looked at her intensely and slowly said, "You're really beautiful. You know that, don't you?" Li Qin only smiled, and Brad traced her body with his hands without touching her.

"What's it like?" Li Qin asked.

"Smoking *ganj*?"

Li Qin chuckled and said, "No. What's New York City like?"

"Parties . . . yeah, lots of parties: bars, clubs, 24/7."

There was a long pause, as Brad recollected the question.

"Oh, yeah, out-freaking-rageous," he added, through an exhale.

"Like Shanghai?"

Brad nodded, but then said, "No. Better. Yeah . . . like, way better than Shanghai. You got to see it."

"Will you take me there?"

"What—Shanghai?"

Li Qin giggled, "No, New York City."

"'Course, Dude . . . like after you graduate or something."

Li Qin kissed him long and deep, and then pushed him onto his back and straddled him.

The next day, Li Qin returned Michael's phone to him (he was about to go out to buy another one), and lied about how she had retrieved it. She didn't stay long at his apartment, making the excuse that her mother was ill, and that she needed to visit her. It seemed plausible to Michael.

During the week, Li Qin saw Brad a couple of times, and made plans to stay the weekend with him. She called Michael and told him that she couldn't see him on Sunday, as was their routine. There were relatives in town for a visit, and she hadn't seen them in years, she told Michael. And, of course, he believed her. She would drop by on Monday for a quick visit, she added.

That weekend Li Qin stayed with Brad, and by Sunday morning she thought, 'So this is what love is really like,' and knew Brad was the one to take her out of China.

Monday morning came too soon.

"I'm going to be busy for a few days. I'll see you on Wednesday, okay?" she whispered into Brad's ear. He was still asleep and didn't respond.

"I'll call you, okay Brad?"

"Okay," he mumbled, stretching, but not opening his eyes. Li Qin kissed him on the cheek, lifted the sheet and took a quick peek, sighed, and then left the apartment.

When Michael saw Li Qin on Monday, she looked strangely preoccupied and somewhat anxious. Thinking it had something to do with her mother, who had been complaining lately of an irritable bowel, he asked unemphatically, "It's your mother, isn't it? Is she alright?"

"Yes, Michael, she's fine. There's something else. We need to talk." She took a deep breath and continued, "Last weekend I was with a boy," she said quickly, while averting.

"What do you mean?"

"I stayed with a boy in his apartment. We slept together."

"What?!" Michael exploded; his face turned beet red and shook like Nixon's.

"Michael, are you okay?"

"No! After—*ahg*—all . . . all this! That psycho-bitch mother of yours, and . . . and having to sneak around all the time? No, absolutely not—I'm not okay!"

"But Michael, I thought you wouldn't care. I thought you'd be happy for me." And, at some level, Li Qin actually thought that Michael would be happy for her, and that he would gladly bow out.

Michael stood glaring into Li Qin's eyes, like looking deep within her soul.

"Didn't you always say that my life was my own, and that you'd respect my choices?" said Li Qin.

"What are you, a moron? We were talking about grad schools in America. Not sleeping around!"

"We only slept in one place." She smiled nervously, hoping Michael would find it humorous. He didn't.

"What's his name?"

"Brad."

"Brad. A foreigner, or is that his English name?" Michael asked.

"A foreigner—an American from New York City," she answered, smiling and slightly bobbing on the balls of her feet. Brad was a trophy!—young, handsome, and from New York City—and Li Qin knew it. There'd be no sneaking around with him. They could be, and would be, publicly seen together and other girls would be so jealous of her.

"American, I should've known." Michael shook his head in disgust. "Was he a good lay? Better than me?"

"What?"

"Did you blow him?"

"What?"

"How many times did you cum?"

"What are you asking, Michael?"

"I don't know." He paused momentarily, embarrassed by his questioning—and then told Li Qin, "Get out of my apartment, slut."

"Slut—what does slut mean?"

"S-L-U-T, look it up!" Michael yelled, as he forcefully pushed her out the door.

"He's beautiful, Michael. You're too old and boring!"

And, Michael slammed the door. "I didn't handle *that* very well," he said out loud. "I need to take a walk," he added, while walking to the wardrobe to fetch his jacket and cap.

(Li Qin was right about one thing: Michael *had* become boring, too paternal, and he knew it. To him she was fragile: physically, but mostly emotionally. He couldn't push the limits with her, like he could others in his past. Above all else, to Michael, Li Qin needed his protection.)

Walking as far as the pond, Michael sat against a barkless, bleached stump at the edge. A fish rose on the glassy surface. Michael doubted whether there would be anyone for him again: a sad fate for a foreigner, jilted in a strange land.

"Now, what am I going to do?" he whispered, pausing, and then said aloud, "You're too old for all this, Michael." He was now 40 years old.

Why did I think I could find someone again, someone like Helene? What I had with her. She was me, my identity. I'll never have that again, never. It would be so easy to give up right now. End it. Be rid of it. Why fight the inevitable? Why wait? Maybe then, Helene and I could be together again.

Night was settling in.

As the eastern sky began to lighten Michael was still there, sitting propped against the barkless, bleached stump at the edge of the pond. In the early morning, just as the day was beginning to break, all was quiet, and the air was an eerie calm. There, he sat reminiscing, his mind uncluttered and free to wander. Presently, his thoughts drifted to Helene. She hadn't visited him in a while, and he wondered why. And, still he waited.

Daybreak brought the cacophony of waterfowl to the pond. A breeding pair of Mandarin ducks waddled past the stump to the edge, gliding smoothly into the water, and joining in the morning discordance. Springtime, it was expected. He'd sat there before to welcome in the day, yet today was different. It brought him only sorrow. It was spring, after all. He had seen himself returning to America, with Li Qin, and starting a family. Now, that was gone.

And where's Helene?

For two weeks, Li Qin and Brad carried on their affair in the city. She skipped afternoon classes almost every day, so she could be at his apartment when he finished teaching. They explored the city. She showed him places to shop and dine that he didn't know existed, and at night he took her to clubs that catered to the international crowd. She met all his friends and their Chinese girlfriends, and felt like a princess with her prince.

It was two weeks of *amour fou.*

On Monday morning, two weeks after the affair began, Li Qin left Brad's apartment, promising that she would see him again on Wednesday.

Later that day, when she knew that he was at lunch, Li Qin phoned Brad. He didn't pick up. Other calls and messages also went unanswered. But, she thought that his phone probably needed to be recharged or was out of money. There had to be a reasonable explanation, and she was left unconcerned.

By Tuesday evening, Li Qin had become frantic.

Early Wednesday morning she went into the city and to his apartment. She knocked and knocked, calling out his name, and then banged on the door hard with her fists. She woke a neighbor, a middle-aged Chinese woman.

"What's all this commotion?"

"I'm looking for the boy that lives here," Li Qin answered, in a quavering voice.

"Big Nose?—he left."

"What do you mean?" asked Li Qin.

"Left, moved out."

"Moved out! When?"

"Monday morning."

"Monday morning?! Oh, no." Panicky, Li Qin sat down on the floor. She began to cry.

"There was girl here yesterday," began the middle-aged Chinese woman. "She was looking for him, too. You should pray you're not pregnant. I have ears, you know," the woman said, while stepping back into her apartment. She sneered slightly and mumbled, "Stupid, naïve girl," and then shut the door.

"Stop calling me that!" Li Qin was tired of everyone calling her stupid and naïve. But, now she knew it was true.

On the bus back to campus, Li Qin recalled something from Saturday night. She and Brad were at a club with friends, when a drunken foreigner that Brad called Jamie—who was wearing eye shadow, rouge, a drab Japanese flight attendant skirt, and open blazer (*sans* white blouse), and black patent leather pumps—staggered over to their table.

"One last blowout before you bail?" Jamie asked Brad.

"No, we're staying 'til closing time. See you later, Jamie," replied Brad.

Jamie turned, stopped, then turned back around, and said, "Oh, I've been meaning to tell you, if you ever get herpes, dab a little white vinegar on the sores; it really works. But, it might take something like two weeks for them to go away."

"I'll keep that in mind," answered Brad.

"Okay, give my regards to Broadway," said Jamie, as he scampered away from the table, casting magical pixie dust into the air, and emitting *a bjjj, bjjj* sound.

What a strange man, thought Li Qin. It didn't make sense to her, what Jamie had said. But, Brad shrugged it off and laughed, and then said, "That's just Jamie. He's always really drunk or really high, and he's kind of crazy, too. Don't pay any attention to him."

(According to Jamie, himself, he was found on campus in one of the southern provinces early one morning horrifically inebriated. Sitting naked against a tree, he was smearing his own feces on his face and torso. Consequently, he was fired. But, within three days, he had found a teaching job at a kindergarten in Harbin. Brad hadn't mentioned that to Li Qin.)

Li Qin could see that it all made perfect sense now. She felt so stupid, so naïve.

Two days later Li Qin was at Michael's door, crying and begging him to take her back.

"Oh Michael, I'm so sorry I hurt you. You're such a sweet, gentle man. I don't know what's wrong with me," she said.

"I don't want you back." He pushed her out the door and shut it.

She pounded on the door. "But, he's gone now, Michael. Please let me in." She started to sob hard.

He opened the door, but stood blocking the doorway.

"You can beat me, if that's what it will take," she screamed, "anything!"

"Beat you?" He made a fist and smirked. She shut her eyes and braced herself, expecting to be flattened.

"No, I'm *not* going to beat you, but as long as you are here . . .," said Michael, grabbing Li Qin by the hair, and dragging her into the apartment.

"Ow!" she cried out, as she reached up and grabbed a hold of his wrist.

Tossing her onto the bed, he lifted her short denim skirt above her waist, and pulled her panties off. Flipping her over and onto her belly, he lifted her waist and pushed her knees forward, elevating her bottom, and spanked her left butt-cheek hard one time.

"Ah!" she cried.

Pulling his sweats down to his knees, he guided his hard cock to her pussy, pushing hard, forcibly with the first thrust. Nowhere. He thrust again equally hard, barely inching in, and then again.

"You're hurting me!" Li Qin cried out.

Michael gripped her pelvis with both hands, pulling her body back, with another thrust and then another. Now buried deep within her, he pounded hard and fast with immense anger and obsession.

"You like banging other men, is that it? What about Andre, huh? What about it?" Michael gasped. Reaching forward, he grabbed her hair with his left hand, lifting her head back (like using a check rein on a horse), and pulled her hair with each forward thrust until all was spent, and he came quickly and loudly. Withdrawing slowly, he rolled over and onto his back.

Staring at the ceiling, his chest heaved. I've got to quit smoking, he thought.

Li Qin rolled to her side and faced Michael, watching his chest rise and fall, quickly at first, but then slowing to normal breathing. They lay silent for a few minutes, and then Li Qin asked, "Who is Andre?"

Michael didn't respond at first, but then cleared his throat and said, "He was one of my teaching assistants in America, a real pretty boy."

Li Qin waited a moment, and then said, "Oh." Then more silence. And, then she said, "I'm sorry, Michael, really I am. But, I'm not Helene."

Michael didn't respond.

"You know something else?"

"What?" answered Michael.

"You'd make a really good Chinese husband," said Li Qin quietly, as she rolled onto her back.

"Sarcasm—wow!—I'm impressed." Michael got up and walked to the kitchen, mumbling, "I bet you don't think I'm so sweet and gentle now, do you?"

He returned with a glass of wine and a cigarette, and walked to the window.

"Li Qin?" He said, while facing the window.

"Yes?" She was lying on her belly now, and looked up at him.

"I don't think I'll ever be able to trust you again."

"I know you're very angry with me, Michael. But, I promise I'll never do anything like that again. Let's start over, shall we?"

"We shan't. I think you should go now," he said, walking to the foot of the bed, and then sitting on it.

"Please, Michael, don't make me go."

"I'm sorry, but you need to leave now," said Michael sternly, but without raising his voice. The anger was gone. But, she was no longer his, and that couldn't be forgotten. Sex mattered to Michael. What was left was anticlimactic and now cliché.

Li Qin retrieved her panties from the floor. They were torn beyond wear. Shaking her head in disgust, she tossed them into her bag.

As she opened the door to leave the apartment, Li Qin stopped, and, without looking at Michael, said, "I can smell perfume in your bed, Michael. It smells like that pretty Russian teacher, the blond one. What's her name?"

"Elena," he said, putting out his cigarette.

"Yes, Elena. Do you know that I once played the piano and sang for her in the music room?"

"What song?"

"'Angel', by Sarah McLachlan. Do you know it?"

"I do. Did Elena enjoy it?"

"She said it was beautiful."

Then, Li Qin glanced over at Michael, paused, and said, "You're a jerk, Michael," and quickly left.

Michael walked back to the window, and finished his glass of wine. He could see Li Qin walking toward the library.

From a stack of books on the windowsill, he picked up a self-made, saddle stitch volume of favorite poems. Flipping quickly through it, he stopped at Cesar Vallejo's *Los Heraldos Negros* (translator omitted), and began to read aloud.

". . . and all of life's experiences become stagnant, like a puddle of guilt, in a daze."

In front of the library, Li Qin stopped, adjusted her skirt, looked back toward the foreign teachers' apartment building, then back to the library, and entered it.

For a week, Li Qin left multiple messages for Michael, explaining that she'd been fooled by a handsome face and a long list of promises. She was caught up in his charm, and in his lies. Stupid, naïve girl, thought Michael.

The last message read:

"Now I know that you were the one all along. I'm sorry, Michael. Love, Li Qin."

Michael didn't reply to any of them.

THE VISITANT

MICHAEL AWOKE ALONE from a night of heavy drinking, with his head pounding and his stomach queasy. A party?—he remembered a party, with a lot of people standing around and chatting. But, he couldn't remember any of them. It was now all a daze. Sliding to the edge of the bed, he sat up and tried to stand. But, he only fell to his knees. Crawling to the desk, he pulled himself to his feet, his legs weak and wobbly. His lower back racked in pain. Two empty bottles of *baijiu* lay on his desk next to a half-empty glass.

(The Songhua River, the great river of Harbin, was polluted with industrial poisons, its canals contaminated with caramel-colored effluents. Old men fished in its stench, and then sold their catches to nearby restaurants. The river was sick and dying.

Like Harbin's waterways, Michael's body was infected by the poisons of the night before. Michael was sick and dying, as well. But, he didn't care. Why was he still in China? He didn't belong there; he didn't belong to anyone there; he could trust no one there. Alienated again, and uncertain of the direction to take, he grew restless, unsettled, and desperate. So, he drank himself to near-death.

But Michael knew his condition was reversible. His body would respond. He would have to want be healthy, though, and that was the first step. He wasn't ready for it, yet.

For the Songhua River the prognosis was doubtful. Its gods had been vacated for science and technology, for the development of a new China. The model was a simple one: achieve development, and then clean up the environment. Was it possible? Could China fix what had been maltreated for so long? Would the Songhua River become another casualty of rapid, unrestrained, non-sustainable development, like the loss of farmlands, underground water supplies, and the destruction of rural-family traditional values and practices?)

Michael had to urinate and maybe vomit. Quickly, he downed the half-empty glass of *baijiu*.

"It's cold in here," he said out loud, and looked to the window to see if it was open. It wasn't.

When Michael pissed into the toilet, his urine was cola colored. "Ah, that can't be good," he said, and staggered back to the bedroom. There, lying in his bed was a young man, with dark, wavy hair, who looked to be in his early to mid-twenties, covered with a blanket to his waist. Michael stood speechless for a moment, thinking it was all a hallucination, but then offered anyway, "Who are you?"

"I'm Darryl. Who are you?"

"Michael. What are you doing in my bed?"

"Trying to sleep, what else? What are you doing in my apartment?"

"You're the one in the wrong apartment, Darryl. I live here."

"No, I do. I've lived here all year."

Michael was sick. He didn't want to argue. Walking to the side of the bed opposite Darryl, he sat on the edge with his back to him.

"Look, Darryl, I'm—

"Were you at the party?" asked Darryl.

"I'm not sure."

"What happened . . . I mean, at the party? What happened at the party? I need to know."

"I don't know. I'm not sure I was even there. But, I do know that I'm going back to bed now," said Michael.

Darryl sat up.

"You're going to have to lea . . .," said Michael, as he turned to look at Darryl. But, Darryl was gone. Michael crawled back into bed, and tried to focus on the overhead light fixture. But, it was spinning. So, he dropped one foot to the floor, and then pulled the covers over his head.

Later in the day, Michael saw Serge on the commons, sitting on a bench and reading a book. His T-shirt was on backwards. Michael didn't question it. Most likely there was a large stain on the front, which was now the back and covered by his blazer, figured Michael.

"Mind if I join you?"

"Be my guest, Michel."

"Thanks." They shook hands, and talked a little about the unseasonably warm afternoon. Then, Michael told Serge about his so-called dream.

"I saw a man lying in my bed this morning," said Michael. "He said his name was Darryl."

"Lucky you!"

"No, it's not like that. What I mean is—

"Yes, Michel, I know what you mean. And, it sounds peculiar."

"So, you don't know any Darryl? I was thinking that it might not have been a dream. Maybe I left my door unlocked." He paused, and then added, "Or, maybe it was the *baijiu*."

Yes, Michel, you do look a bit bedraggled today. You shouldn't drink alone, my dear. When one drinks alone, he drinks too much."

"So, you don't know any Darryl?" Michael asked again. "I've asked some other teachers, and nobody knows a Darryl."

"No, I don't think I know such a person, either," said Serge, thinking about it momentarily. But then, he added, "Oh, but wait a minute—yes! There was a Darryl here some years ago—maybe eight or nine years ago, maybe more now—a young American, and I think he lived in your apartment. Yes, I'm certain of it now. But, not to worry, he's dead."

"What!—dead?"

"Yes, he fell out a window. I remember: he was having a party—it seems to me that it was this time of year; many teachers and students were there—and he was sitting on the sill, and then (blowing a raspberry), he was gone. Six floors down. *Il est mort*. But, I wasn't there. I didn't see it."

"So, the person I saw was a ghost?"

"Yes, it does sound very much like you've seen a ghost, my dear!"

"That's weird. Usually I only see—

"Yes, it is quite special," interrupted Serge. "I have never seen one, myself. I thought I did once, but it was only my reflection in a mirror."

On a Thursday in late June, Li Qin graduated. That night on campus, and in the city, there were parties, a lot of them. Michael had been invited to some, but declined all invitations. Li Qin would be at one or more, he knew, and he didn't want to run into her. It would be awkward, especially if she were drunk.

Next morning Michael went jogging at 6 A.M., as he had done every morning that month. As he returned to campus, and was nearing the foreign faculty residence building, he met Li Qin exiting the main door. Their eyes met.

"Walk of shame?" he asked, mockingly.

She quickly looked down and hurried past Michael, without saying a word. Li Qin didn't know what he meant by it. But, by the tone of his voice and his facial expression, she knew it couldn't be good.

Li Qin had stayed the night with one of his colleagues, Michael was certain of it. But, which one—did he really want to know?

That was the last time he saw her on campus.

That summer Michael was one of a few foreign teachers that stayed on campus. Three of his officemates were traveling, and Serge had returned to France permanently. It was rumored that he was setting up a household for a new bride, his fifth, though he hadn't mentioned any of it to Michael.

THE OFFER

MICHAEL RETURNED FROM his biweekly shopping trip and checked his emails. Normally, he checked them first thing in the morning. But, that morning, he had left his apartment in a hurry, wanting to return home early enough to still feel energetic. There was a movie he had been dying to watch; lately, he had been falling asleep midway through most other movies.

There, waiting for him, was an email from Loch. It was relatively short and to the point, as one expected of Loch, since he hated all forms of electronic communications. And, Michael felt privileged that he had made the effort to contact him personally and electronically.

The email read:

"Michael, we have two openings for The Stonington (a Writer-in-Residence program)—one for the fall and the other for the spring. I've nominated you for either one. You're a shoo-in. And, I've already spoken to the chair and provost about offering you a tenured position, given your experience and publications, once you have completed the residency. We'll be interviewing for it shortly, probably within the month. Are you interested?"

Michael replied:
"Can you give me more specifics on the position?"

And Loch did. After perusing the specifics, Michael then asked for a week to decide, and Loch agreed.

There were positive things about the position:

He would be in the same city as Loch and his wife, Becky.

He could use the time to polish his book-length manuscript of short poems that he had recently finished.

He could finish the first-draft of his novella (*would it ever be finished?*).

And, there would be the energy and intellect of young American minds. That was one thing he did miss, since leaving American academia.

But, after much deliberation and the many miles of the many walks that week, Michael declined the interview, and thus the Writer-in-Residence and faculty positions. There would be questions, prying he figured.

The interview:
Q: "Why did you leave academia, in the first place?"
A: "It sucked."
Q: "Why China?"
A: "There weren't any openings in Nebraska or the Virgin Islands."

Q: "Here (CV), it lists numerous awards. Some appear to be . . . dare I say, minority scholarships, and the like. Are they? That is to say, is my assumption correct?"

A: "Dare I answer, 'Yes'?"

(Interviewer): "Thank you for being frank."

(Michael): "You're welcome, and my name is Michael."

Q (Second Interviewer): "But, you don't look like a minority."

Q (Michael): "What does 'a minority' look like?"

A (Interviewer): "I don't want to go there. I mean, come on, you know the   ramifications of such an—

Q (Third Interviewer): "Just to be sure, I suggest a blood test. Are you open to that?"

A: "Not at all."

Q (First Interviewer): "Ah, huh! Hmm, I see, I see. That speaks volumes."

Michael chuckled.

If he accepted the position, he would have to try to avoid the faculty altogether. But, there would be mandatory meetings and social events, and he would have to prepare for, and protect himself from, anticipated criticisms. The office environment had the potential of becoming unbearable. No, it was more than potential; it was a certainty. For one, he could never shake the stigma of having taught in China. It would follow him, forever. Nothing is worth ridicule, or worse, pity. *Nothing!* And, that is what it would be like; he knew how American academics were, inherently. He had been there before. *I won't be fooled again.* He liked China, and he would continue to teach in China. It was the only place he knew of, where he could effortlessly teach a few courses, and disappear in the mediocrity of it all. He was a "nobody" in China, invisible, and he liked it. In China, he could write. And, he *was* writing. When he couldn't teach anymore, or didn't want to teach anymore, or if he had to leave China for whatever reason, then, but only then, would he go someplace else. Maybe it would be America. But, now was not the time.

"No. It would be all the same problems, all over again," he said aloud to his computer monitor. He had gained a different perspective from afar, and it had shown him the truth, and convinced him of the obvious.

Michael emailed Loch:

"Sorry, Old Man, I've decided against it. Thank you for the opportunity. Being nominated for the prestigious Stonington is an honor in itself, and I'm grateful to you. Good luck, and all my best to Becky, Michael."

AVERY

THE SUMMER MONTHS were marked by two separate, yet indirectly connected events: the engagement of Li Qin, and Michael's meeting Avery.

Over the summer, Li Qin's mother, with the assistance of friends and relatives, bought Li Qin a government English teaching job at an elementary school in Jinan City (costing 140,000 RMB). It was the city in which Li Qin's family had originated, and was still home to her maternal grandparents. Part of the agreement was for Li Qin to marry an educational administrator, some ten years her senior and recently widowed, with the provincial education bureau there. There were familial ties with the man and his family, though Li Qin had never met him. Li Qin's mother thought it was the best or only way for her to keep Li Qin from seeing Michael, or any foreigner for that matter (Li Qin had told her mother about Brad), and leaving China to become a "prostitute" in America.

Li Qin emailed Michael, explaining the circumstances of the arrangement, and that she had no feelings toward the man whatsoever. But, her hands were tied, and she foresaw no possible way out of it, other than fleeing the country. Michael didn't reply.

For Michael, the summer months settled into a rather mundane, though comfortable routine. Every morning he slept late and, after a quick breakfast of fruit, yogurt, and boiled eggs, walked to his office to read for one hour. The office was quiet and still cool before noon. Afterward, Michael returned to his apartment to plan his day.

On a hot afternoon in mid-August, Michael walked to a nearby coffee shop. He had work to do: proofreading one of his graduate student's manuscript of poems, and couldn't do it without caffeine (and maybe a glass or two of wine, later in the day). In the dimly lit coffee shop, with good, eclectic international music playing, Michael sat at a small, round table for two. It was near a window for light, and close enough to the speakers to hear the music. There, he set about finishing the manuscript. Consumed by his work, he noticed nothing else around him.

When he heard the Johnny Cash rendition of the Beatles' "There Are Places I Remember", Michael took a break from his task, finished his first cup of coffee (an *Americano* that had become cold), and lifted it to order another. The waiter nodded. It was then that Michael noticed an attractive Chinese woman, sitting at a table not far from his. A round, pretty face that radiated peacefulness and confidence, she looked to be about thirty-five. But, he always had problems judging women's ages, especially Asian women. She was probably older.

She smiled at Michael, and he smiled back.

The woman stood up and walked to his table.

"May I join you?" she asked. Her pronunciation was impeccable.

"Certainly," answered Michael, gathering the loose pages of the manuscript together, and stacking them to one side.

"I'm Avery."

Michael introduced himself. They flirted and chatted for a few minutes about everything and nothing, and kept it all very light.

But then, Avery decided to dig a little deeper.

"A person's eyes show his true feelings, Michael."

"What do you mean by that?"

"There's sadness in your eyes," she said.

"Oh . . . it's complicated." Michael sighed, thinking: 'that obvious, huh?'

"So, tell me about it. Maybe I can help."

"It's really quite personal."

With a little more prodding (though, it didn't take much), Michael briefly explained his relationship with Li Qin and their breakup.

"I lost it. I called her a slut, and—

"You were upset," Avery interjected. "It's understandable."

"Still, it's no excuse. But, you see, I have this past."

"We all do, Michael. But, this kind of relationship is never easy. When I was at Columbia—

"You were at Columbia?"

"Yes, for one of my master's."

"That's a very good school."

"Yes, I know. That's why I was there."

"I'm impressed."

"Thank you, but permit me to tell my story."

"Sorry. Please continue."

"At Columbia, I too had an affair with a professor. But, I was only a girl then, an inexperienced girl. I bored him. We had nothing to talk about. So, we had sex—and let me tell you it was really good sex—but that was all." She paused, and then added, with a crooked grin, "He was into Tantric."

"Lucky you!"

"I prefer to think: lucky him," laughed Avery. "And afterward, he would read poetry to me, mostly Dylan Thomas, but sometimes Yeats, and we'd listen to Irish folk music. He wasn't Irish, but I think he wanted to be an Irish poet. There's something so . . . so dangerous in that."

Michael was amused *and* amazed. Avery was different, open, and confident. But, he had already known that America could do that to a foreign woman, given enough time. After all, he had experienced American academia, and had met other foreign women who had studied there, though none of them were Chinese. He extrapolated.

He asked, "Have you ever noticed that on St. Patrick's Day everyone claims to be Irish? But, on *Cinco de Mayo*, nobody but Mexicans claims to be Mexican?"

"Sinkhole, my . . . what?"

"*Cinco de Mayo*—it's a national holiday of Mexico."

"Oh yes, I remember it now."

"Okay. So, getting back to your pseudo–Irish-poet-boyfriend, what happened between you two?"

"I ended it—too many rituals. And, at the same time, I met a boy my own age."

"Was he American?"

"No, he was Chinese, from Beijing, studying at New York University. Film, I recall. Anyway, we could be free, loose. We weren't en . . . en . . . what's the word?"

"Encumbered?"

"Yes, that's it."

"Encumbered by what?"

"By our ages, our experiences, our lifestyles, our beliefs . . . everything, I guess. We felt we belonged together."

"How long were you there?"

"In America?—about seven years, altogether: two for my master's, and then, for the next five years, at Hunter College; I taught there. I loved it."

"Why did you return to China?"

"Filial obligations, of course—why else would a young, extremely successful, beautiful Chinese woman return?" Avery reflected for a moment, and then added, "But now, I'm happy I returned, Michael. I have a good life here. That's not to say I wouldn't go back to America, at some other time. But, for right now, I'm content."

It was puzzling to Michael, in that he thought everyone in China wanted to live in America.

They sat quietly for a moment, and then Avery returned to the previous topic, "Okay, Michael, I'm going to get down and dirty here: Chinese culture is very complex, but simple at the same time. I don't know if your girlfriend loved you, or was just using you. But, I do know that she acted like a normal girl her age. It's as simple as that.

"Chinese girls are not at all *that* mysterious, really. Like girls from every culture, Chinese girls want to have fun, especially before they are married. And, when they do marry, it's for financial security, not love.

"You can't possess what has free will, Michael, nor would you want to. I certainly could never be possessed and controlled. Possessing her would only lead to anguish—yours, not hers. And, you are not going to change Chinese culture, either. So don't even try.

"Her mother?—she only acted like a traditional Chinese mother. She needed to protect her daughter and herself. Her daughter and husband will become her old-age pension.

"There's something else, and it's you. One big difference between your culture and Chinese culture is that we march to a drum that's not so dif . . . what's that saying?"

"March to the beat of a different drum?"

"Yes, that's it. But, in China, it's different: we all march to the beat of the same drum. You're middle-aged and living like you are twenty. Your idea of being free-spirited is seen here as objectionable.

"But don't worry, Michael, you *are* still young, regardless of your age. I can see it in the way you carry yourself—those broad shoulders!—in that crooked smile, and those mischievous, yet sad, sad eyes," Avery said, with a daring expression.

"Thanks, but these broad shoulders and long arms make it very difficult to find shirts that fit. And shoes?—I won't even go there."

Avery peaked beneath the table at Michael's feet: "Long arms, long legs, and big feet— how intriguing!" She giggled, and then continued: "Okay, on to something else, but kind of related. A few years ago, an American scholar like you came to the university—the Normal University, where I teach—to lecture." There was a glint in her eyes.

"Was he your lover?" Michael asked, with a grin.

"I don't kiss and . . . and . . . talk."

"Tell."

"Yes. I don't kiss and tell. Anyway, instead of embracing him, some teachers told their students that he couldn't be a true scholar, in that a scholar would never leave America to come to China to teach. That's really insulting, to both him and our country. Is China not good enough for foreign scholars? Anyway, it was very difficult for him here. He was snubbed! He left after one semester. He wasn't a fake, like so many foreign teachers in China. He only wanted an adventure, a life less ordinary."

"Okay, now back to *my* predicament, what I should do?" Michael asked.

"Simple: forgive your ex-girlfriend. Forgiveness is such a powerful thing—you'll feel better. And, you must move on. Lose the attachment! If you want a Chinese girlfriend, then find yourself an older Chinese woman, like a professor or doctor. Or, better yet, find yourself a westerner. It would be hard for a Chinese family to accept you, Michael. We haven't progressed that far yet. And, you don't speak our language. It's vital. You need to be able to communicate with the family of a potential girlfriend.

"One last thing: in a breakup, you need a sense of humor. It's essential. So chin up, okay?"

Michael smiled with his eyes and nodded.

The coffee was gone, but they were enjoying themselves and didn't want to leave. The conversation turned to other, less personal matters. In time, Michael said: "I could use a glass of wine, how about you?"

"Wine in mid-afternoon? Hmm, yes, that actually sounds like a very good idea. But, we can go to my place to drink a bottle, if you would rather."

"Okay, that sounds even better. First, though, let me finish these last two poems. They're quatrains, so it won't take me too long. Then, I'll be ready to leave."

Avery waved over the waiter for the check.

Michael awoke to diffused sunlight through milky-white, gauze curtains, and quietly slipped out of bed, pulling on his boxers and T-shirt. Picking up *100 Ancient Chinese Poems* from the nightstand, he tiptoed to a bedroom chair next to a window, sat down, and opened the book to somewhere near the middle.

Softly, he began reading aloud "The Plum Blossoms", a Song Dynasty poem, by Wang Anshi, and translated by Wang Jianzhong:

In the nook of a wall a few plum sprays

Blossom alone on the bleak winter days.

From afar, I see they cannot be snows,

For the stealthy breath of perfume hither flows.

(Later that day, Avery told him that the poem was about the gallant attribute of bravery, with probable political connotations. A Chinese scholar once told Michael that in all of writing there is politics. He disagreed, but knew that if he argued his point, it would be considered a political stance. Michael was content in finding the aesthetics within poems.)

While he whispered the poem, Avery stirred and then sat up, yawning. Seeing Michael sitting by the window, she smiled, and then ambled to the bathroom. In the soft light, Michael could see the beauty of her roundness. One couldn't say she was plump or pudgy; she was simply round, with slightly larger than usual breasts for a Chinese woman. At first, Michael thought they had been augmented. Few women in China had breasts as large, and those that did were generally overweight. Avery wasn't overweight, and he had discovered from the night before that her breasts were naturally large.

"You look beautiful naked in the light," Michael called out.

"Tell me something I don't know," she replied from the bathroom. Michael chuckled. He was enamored by Avery.

When she returned, covered by a blue, silk kimono, she said, "I need coffee, what about you?"

"More than the breath of life itself," he replied.

"Oh, all I've got is instant—Nescafe. Is that okay?"

Michael nodded yes, and then said, "I like these poems."

"They're good, aren't they?" replied Avery.

"Yeah, I've studied Tang Dynasty poems before, as a grad student, but not Song poems. Now, I'm rereading *300 Tang Poems*. I remember thinking back in grad school how incredible they were; I still do."

"It all depends on translation," said Avery.

"True."

"Of course, you've read Du Fu and Li Bai," said Avery.

"Yes, I like them both, but I especially like Wang Wei," answered Michael.

"Oh, a landscape poet; he's good too. But, I have to tell you, Li Bai is our celebrated—or is the word quintessential?—Tang Dynasty poet."

"He can be both, and I know. But, I always tend to favor the underdog. It's a tribal-thing, I guess," answered Michael.

It was mid-morning now. Michael, still in his boxers and T-shirt, and Avery, in her kimono, sat at the kitchen table, sipping coffee, eating bread, and talking. The conversation returned to ancient Chinese poetry.

"What I like about the Tang Dynasty poems, and those Song Dynasty poems that I just read, is that they have an essence of nature about them; that is to say, nature is mentioned in them: seasons, trees, rivers, mountains, rain, things like that. They are kind of haiku-like. Indian poetry—I should say, American Indian poetry—has that same essence, too."

"You studied Indian poetry, right? I remember saying something about that last night."

"Yes, I did, and other indigenous peoples' poetry, as well."

"Sounds fascinating," said Avery.

"For me it *was* fascinating. The commonalities, and not so much the differences, were most interesting to me. I think they're all, at some ethereal level, connected—connected to their lands.

"Poetry exists in its own language, its own form. That's the beauty of it. In high school, I taught myself Spanish, so I could hear how Cesar Vallejo's poems were supposed to sound. I can only assume that the poems of indigenous peoples must be so beautiful, in their own languages. How could they not be? Unfortunately, I could only read English translations of them. I don't think English is a beautiful language."

They laughed.

"You're a very passionate person, Michael. I think that's a good thing," said Avery.

The two sat quietly for a while, with Avery thinking about Michael's enthusiasm for poems, and Michael thinking about his years in graduate school. Those had been such amazing years, when he and Helene were studying poetry, and writing poems together—hers, so wonderfully crafted; his, so raw and poignant. There wasn't any bickering or criticizing, only total support for each other's work.

"Last night you said something about your father, and it confused me," said Avery, bringing them back to the present.

"About Frenchie?—I hope I didn't lie. I was a little drunk," said Michael. Avery chuckled.

"You said that he didn't fit into this world, that he was an old soul. But, I don't know what that means."

"Frenchie lived by the seasons. He was called a real *Bois Brule*, by the old men of my village. He was a trapper, for one thing. Not many people trap these days. But, there were other things, too. I guess the best way to describe Frenchie is to say that he lived by the old ways."

"Were your ancestors hunter-gatherers?"

"Of course, but I think everybody's ancestors were hunter-gathers, at one time," answered Michael.

"No, what I meant was—

"I know what you meant. And, yes, he hunted, and I—

"You hunted, too!" Avery said, excitedly.

"I actually did, mostly for ruffed grouse—we called them partridge—with Frenchie, when I was a boy. But, I did shoot one buck."

"Buck?"

"A whitetail buck—a male deer. I lost my virginity that same night," said Michael, laughingly.

"Oh, intrigue! Do tell."

"Well . . . let's see: I was walking home from the A&P Store—I'd worked the afternoon shift—when Jinni drove up, and—

"Hey Dipstick," shouted Billy, from inside the cab of Jinni's pickup. "Want to go hunting?"

"Season's over," answered Michael.

"Not for us, it ain't." The four in the cab laughed. "We're heading out to Old Man Leveque's place. He'll let us hang one in his garage, if we give him the back straps."

"Yeah, I'm in." With a big grin, Michael crammed himself into the cab.

Out at Old Man's Leveque's, they unloaded the snowmobiles, and Michael climbed on the back of Billy's Ski-Doo. They sped out to the east 40, an empty cow pasture.

"Ever shot a deer before," Billy called back to Michael, who was desperately clutching the 30.06 with one hand, and a side rail with the other, hoping beyond all measure that the ride would soon end.

"Never," he shouted.

"You're a virgin!" Billy laughed. "Well, tonight's the night. Still some bucks with horns. I saw one cross this morning, down by the river, this side of St. Jacque's place. But, we can't hunt there, too many houses. It had a really big rack. Maybe, you'll get a trophy tonight. Maybe even Jinni. She's a trophy." He laughed again.

"Jinni?"

"Yeah. She likes you, man. She thinks you're cute."

Michael and Billy sat at the edge of the field at the tree line, concealed in a stand of blue spruce, and waited in the still, starlit, subzero evening. It was this side of 7 P.M. In the moonlight, they watched the edge of a cedar stand, along the side of a swale. Presently deer—all does—meandered into the hayfield, digging in the snow for grass, some 20 of them.

"If we don't see a buck pretty soon, take one of them does. It's too cold tonight to sit much longer," whispered Billy. Still, they waited.

About the time Billy was going to give Michael permission to shoot a doe that had come within 50 yards of them, Billy noticed a big lone deer, walking cautiously out of the cedars.

"Wait . . . right there," whispered Billy, slowly pointing to the far left of the herd. "Give me the gun." Michael handed him the rifle. Through the scope, Billy could see it was a big buck.

"Whoa!" whispered Billy, and he handed back the rifle. "He's a dandy."

Michael raised the rifle and saw the buck. Its rack was wider than it was tall.

"Want me to take him now?"

"No. He's looking this way. Wait 'til he puts his head down."

The buck was now about 100 yards out. Billy whispered, "Okay, he's broadside. Aim just behind the front shoulders . . . wait, wait, he's turning."

The buck faced the two, lifting its head high.

"This is your only chance. Aim just below the chin. Be quick about it!"

"Okay." Michael placed the crosshairs below the chin of the buck and squeezed:

Ka-BOOM

The buck dropped, and the does bounded into the cedars.

"You got him, man, you got him!" He punched Michael in the shoulder.

Billy gutted the buck in a matter of minutes. He was good at it; his family being one of the few left on the rez that lived off of venison nearly year round. It was healthier than commodities. Michael watched in awe.

"Come on, we'll tie him to the back, and drag him out to Old Man Leveque's garage," said Billy.

The garage was warm, the wood stove popping. Everybody, now a group of about a dozen, was drinking beer, talking and laughing, and jamming to Black Sabbath.

Old Man Leveque stepped out of the house and into the garage. Seeing Billy and Michael skinning the buck, he said, "Nice buck, eh? Who got him?"

"Michael," said everyone, and then pointed to him. Michael grinned proudly.

"Michael, eh?" Old Man Leveque approached Michael closely, and looked him square in the eye.

"You Frenchie's boy?"

"Yes, Sir."

"Thought so. You're the spitting image of Frenchie. Good job, my boy. Now, somebody get the grill going. I'm hungry for some steaks," said Old Man Leveque. Then, taking Michael aside, he said, "Frenchie was a good man, a real *Bois Brule*— ain't many like him, no more. You could do worse, my boy." And, then he whispered, "Go wash up, and for crissakes talk to Jinni."

—Michael paused for a long moment, sipped his coffee, and then said to Avery, "There's really nothing to tell," in a sad, reflective kind of way.

"Oh, come on," she pleaded.

"No, I think it's best left between Jinni and me," replied Michael, and Avery gave him a pouty look.

Michael continued: "My ancestors were from the Great Lakes. They were great fishermen." He paused, then added, "And storytellers, too."

"Storytellers?"

"Yeah, it's a traditional-thing. Frenchie used to tell me stories, when I was a boy. There's one, especially—I wish I could remember it now—it was about a pig on a great journey to find soup. It must have been a metaphor. Frenchie said it was my very own story. But, for the life of me, I can't remember it."

"It'll come back to you. What about nowadays? Are they still telling stories?"

"Yeah, still about the same—no, that's not right—the stories are getting lost. The elders can't remember all of them anymore, and the children are only interested in iPhones and Facebook, anyway." Michael paused, and then added, "Technology is making the world lazy, stupid, and socially inept. Creativity is all but gone. And, identity is now the brand a person chooses."

"You sound angry."

"No. I don't think I'm angry. I am sad, though. I wish kids today could experience what I experienced in Crooked River— in the woods, on the lakes, the rivers—with Frenchie. There was that ever-present sweet, pure scent of wet earth, and always a story to be told. I knew tradition, for those few short years I was in Crooked River. I knew what it was like to be a member of a community, where all participants lived interdependently—a man-land interdependence—a symbiotic relationship in the natural world."

"So, you're saying that technology is all to blame?" asked Avery.

"Not all, but partially . . . yes, of course, it's to blame. How can the elders remember stories, when there's no one to tell them to? But, parenting is also to blame. There are a lot of social problems, nowadays, like drugs and alcohol, neglect and abuse. I shouldn't say nowadays, like it's only been the present generation. It's been going on for a long time. Basically, what it comes down to is a breakdown of traditional standards and values. It's anomie."

Michael reflected for a moment, and then added, "It's not easy for families in Crooked River. America has become a very stressful place. I don't blame anybody, really I don't. Everybody is trying to survive the best way they can. But, sometimes, their best way isn't a very healthy one. They anesthetize to cope with what they have to work with, which is pretty much *nada*. There's cultural memory there, like the smell of October, stirring their restless souls. It's generational."

"That's really sad," said Avery. They both sat silent for minute, and then she continued, "You said before that your ancestors were great fisherman. What about fishing these days?"

"The government highly regulates fishing now."

"It should be the government's job to take care of its people, not overburden them. You should be free to fish."

"That's true, but not all of it's bad. Some regulation *is* needed. The fisheries must be protected from greed.

"But, what it really has to do with is money. Money drives the system and decisions are made on how much revenue could be lost or gained," he added.

"It's the same in China, maybe in every country," said Avery. "Do you think you'll ever return to America?"

"Probably."

"Will you fish?"

Michael couldn't answer the question. He didn't know. Returning to America, to Crooked River and fishing were one and the same for Michael. The thought of returning was always there. But, was he too far removed from his homeland now, and that way of life? Would he be lost, a bumbling fool: that ironic guy that returns after years of separation, and then tries desperately to fit in, but never can?

And, of course, there was Maud to contend with.

Avery stood up from the table and walked to the bathroom, slipping out of the kimono on the way. Hanging it on a hook on the bathroom door, she then turned to Michael and said, "It's time for a quickie and a nap."

Michael walked to the foot of the bed, pulled his T-shirt up and over his head, and slipped his boxers off. Avery pushed him down into a sitting position, straddled his lap, and then sat down facing him.

"You really like it on top, don't you?"

"Yes. That way I can guide you to . . . guide your . . ." She reached down, and stroked his erection.

"My penis?"

"Yes, your penis. I can guide your penis to where it gives me the most stimulation. That way I can have orgasms."

"Yeah, I figured that out last night," said Michael.

"You're a good lover, Michael. That's why you're still here."

"And you're a domineering lover, Avery," said Michael, with a chuckle.

It was mid-afternoon and Michael and Avery awoke in bed, entangled in each other.

"Michael, tell me an Indian children's story; one you do remember," said Avery.

"Okay, let me see . . . yeah, I've got one."

A long time ago, three porcupine brothers lived together in a wigwam by the big lake. They were happy there. One cold, winter's morning, after breakfast, the three brothers sat next to their fire, smoking tobacco and talking, when one spotted a wolf circling the camp. Run! shouted one brother. Hide! shouted another. One brother ran into the wigwam and pulled a blanket over himself. One brother dug deep into the snow. And one brother climbed a tree. The wolf, hungry from days without food, sneaked into the wigwam and, sniffing about, found the first brother and gobbled him up. Then the wolf stepped outside, and lay down next to the fire and fell asleep. When he awoke, he was ravenous. He sniffed about the snow and, in finding the second brother, gobbled him up. Feeling satisfied, the wolf lay down next to the fire and fell asleep. When the wolf awoke, he was famished. He sniffed about the tree and, in smelling the third brother, jumped as high as he could to reach the branch on which the brother porcupine was sitting. But the wolf couldn't reach the branch, no matter how hard he tried. He wanted to climb the tree, but he was told that wolves don't climb trees, so he didn't even try. The wolf soon lost interest in the third brother, and walked off into the woods, far from the wigwam.

"So, what do you think of the story?"

"An allegory, huh?" answered Avery.

"Okay, yeah, I guess you could say that. But, what's the lesson?"

Avery thought about it for a short while and then answered, "It has to do with protecting yourself from danger. But, I suspect there's more."

"For me—and it's really up to each listener to find his own meaning in it—it's more about protecting oneself, seeking shelter out of reach of a potential, ominous consequence."

"What's your 'ominous consequence'?"

"Complacency," answered Michael without hesitation. "What else?"

THE WEEKEND

AS HE THOUGHT about Li Qin, Michael found a curious comfort in knowing that she had experienced young love, even though she was used and deceived. She got to experience those feelings of immediately falling madly in love, of strolling along a street holding hands and laughing at the rest of the world, of sitting in coffee shops totally oblivious to what was going on around them, and of having unrestrained, adventurous sex in mid-afternoon.

With Michael, theirs was a physically confined relationship. It had been mature sex from the start; sex perfected by years of practice. It was as if Li Qin had jumped right into the middle of something mid-life. It wasn't bad sex. It was just calculated sex, with ritualistic foreplay in the shower. The affair was destined to end, when passion and spontaneity faded. And, both had been gone for a while.

He wondered, had he purposely though subconsciously chased her away? Had drama become too much for him, passion too little? Instead of being his lover, had she become a distraction, an interruption, an aggravation, a responsibility?

Had they stayed together only because the alternative was aloneness and lonesomeness?

The last week of August Michael emailed Li Qin. It simply read: "I want to see you as soon as possible, unless you're already married."

Li Qin phoned him immediately.

"No, I'm not married yet. The wedding is planned for Spring Festival. So, yes, let's get together."

"How about next Friday?" offered Michael.

"Sounds really good. Shall I book a room?"

"No, let's find one after I arrive," he answered.

Michael planned the weekend. He'd spare no expense.

They stayed at the five-star Crown Plaza in the most expensive suite available, and dined in some of the finest restaurants in Jinan City. Nothing about it was comfortable or predictable.

Their last night, while drinking wine at English Corner—a favorite coffee shop among expats—Michael and Li Qin promised each other that everything was forgotten, and that this was their new beginning.

"We'll live in Paris, won't we Michael?"

"Anywhere you want."

"It's going to be so romantic."

Michael smiled, when he saw the longing in Li Qin's eyes.

"Michael, what's that saying you once told me, something like: 'love is love, only when it comes back to you'?"

"Yeah, that's pretty close."

"You're back, Michael. I knew you'd come back."

At that moment Michael averted. But then, raising his glass, he toasted, "To Paris and romance," and managed a quick, though feigned smile.

On a cool and overcast Monday morning, their five-star weekend in Jinan City ended on a platform at the train station, with a quick kiss. It was 05:40 when the train pulled away. Underdressed and shivering, Li Qin watched the train disappear around a curve, and then rushed home to ready herself for the day of teaching ahead of her; the school year for her had already begun.

And, Michael slept all the way to Beijing.

PART TWO: THE DISTRACTION

THE TRUTH

THE TRAIN FROM BEIJING arrived in Harbin, and Michael awoke to the crowd pushing its way down the aisle to disembark the train. On the platform, the crowd maneuvered its way to the exit doors and onto the street. Michael thought about calling Avery. She would certainly meet him, and then maybe he could convince her to let him stay the night at her place. He didn't want to be alone. But, a former student recognized Michael amongst the crowd, and asked if he'd like to share a taxi back to campus. Michael agreed.

By early evening, Michael was home, satiated, showered, and in his sweats, standing before his apartment window—the one overlooking the common, the lights on the walkways, and the view of the pond—sipping a glass of wine.

Each new academic year brought an influx of fresh foreign teachers to China, some with their many, though similar, tales of woe. Fall semester, 2008 (and possibly forever, thereafter) was an exception, in that it brought a throng of them. Michael, a quiet thinker and appearing consumed by his own past misfortunes (they had seen that disheartening look before, in their own mirrors), found himself an easy target for their depressing stories. Not only were their stories depressing, but some were outlandish lies (*no you're not; the State Department doesn't hire idiots or ugly people*). Their paranoia and obsessions with conspiracy theories and the paranormal (mostly UFOs and ghosts) were too cliché, and Michael found he could use nothing from them in his own storytelling. Michael couldn't empathize, because he couldn't relate. So, in midstream of their one-sided conversations, he walked off and avoided them forever after.

But, there *was* one that intrigued Michael; his name was Julio, and he was a Hispanic-American man, in his mid- to late-50s. With shoulder-length, grey-white hair and a white goatee (and, with a cigarette always in hand, when not physically in the classroom), he looked well beyond his years. Michael stopped Julio on the bridge over the pond to ask for a smoke; he obliged, and then offered a sampling of his story:

"I'd become a slave to my education," he said. "Being an educated man only served to make me work harder, longer hours—time spent away from my family—and I was totally stressed out. The harder I worked the further *we* got behind, and the deeper in debt we'd become. It was too much for my wife. She finally divorced me. But, it was long in the making, and I don't blame her. A woman of her generation still needs attention. I just don't know why she stayed so long.

"Education at best instilled in me an internal satisfaction, in that I could understand what I read. But there it ended for me.

"And then, one day, as I was walking to a lecture hall to deliver a lecture on a topic, in which I had little interest, I stopped half-way, turned around, and walked back to my office. It was a moment of clarity. I wrote my letter of resignation, handed it to the chair, packed up my office, and went home. The sad thing is that most people, I think, have that moment of clarity, but their mortgages, their car payments, their children's piano lessons take precedence. They continue on with their depressing lives, thinking that it is expected, that it is normal, that it is what they're obliged to do. But *it*, of course, affects their job performance, their relationships, their health. It certainly did mine.

"It's like here, with Chinese men, and all the fervor of getting rich. Is there a deadline fast approaching for becoming wealthy? If they hesitate, for one minute, will they lose out? It's all so immediate here. Nothing is planned out for the future. So, they stay in this (looking toward the hazy skyline) unhealthy murk, sleep for an hour or two in their offices at night, see their families for a couple of hours once a week. And, daily, there are the business luncheons and dinners, with their mass consumption of liquor and cigarettes, and prostitutes later in the evening. Oftentimes, the interpreters/translators *are* the prostitutes; it's like an implied part of their job description. As long as it's a part of their job, they don't consider themselves prostitutes, just interpreters/translators. It's a crazy life here, and they're all killing themselves living it; it's kind of like what I was doing in America, but without the prostitutes.

"So, in the end, I chose to make a difference in this world—'my own little Peace Corps'—but without the government's intrusiveness. I chose ethics over money, and it has made all the difference. *This* has replaced *it*, and I've been doing this for more than a decade now.

"And, there's atonement, which I won't go into." And he didn't.

Michael had heard something about Julio being in Vietnam (and parts thereabouts), during the war. There was something there that he didn't want to divulge; Michael could see it in his eyes. Whatever it was, it was a part of him that no one would or could understand, something that was personal, and something that would be forever his. It was locked away. It belonged only to Julio. It would be buried with him.

Over the semester, Michael went out of his way to strike up conversations with Julio, but he was always guarded. They talked about the weather, food and drink, and beautiful women. But, whenever Michael asked about his home, family, and even interests or hobbies, he was met with, "There's not a whole lot to tell." Michael theorized that it had to do with either his war experience or family life, possibly both, in that he thought it best to keep others at a distance, so as not to get attached. The whole expat experience in China was transient. People were continually coming and going. One could avoid being hurt, if he remained detached.

Or, maybe Julio was a middle child, thought Michael.

So, Michael never really got to know Julio, but his kind was more common than not. He had thought that Julio could take the place of Serge, a friend and confidant, but such was not the case.

When the semester ended, Julio left Harbin for someplace in Cambodia (or was it Laos?). Atonement, Michael reasoned. He could only imagine what must have happened to Julio in the war. He heard nothing from or of Julio, thereafter.

For the few years that Michael had been in China, he noticed a pattern among most new recruits. By month two, culture shock had already set in. McDonald's or KFC became their second home, and there they huddled in pairs or groups over coffee. When they (and this was only a few of them) had finally mustered enough courage to patronize an *actual* Chinese restaurant, they might be found periodically in a nearby noodle or dumpling restaurant, drinking themselves blind on cheap beer. Forming a bond of solidarity among other malcontents, they complained that China was nothing like America (or wherever they were from), and argued fervently and embarrassingly loud that everyone but they, including other foreign teachers, were crazy. They reveled in the notion that they weren't alone, considering themselves the normal ones. To them, all other foreigner teachers were no different, but were in denial. Or, and this was Michael's favorite, the other foreign teachers were spies for the university.

A few set off on a "midnight run", as expats liked to call it, for parts unknown, about mid-semester. They left on a weekend or long holiday, taking only a few of their possessions. (They had brought far too much, thinking that China was going to be their new beginning. They planned to stay for the long-term, marry a Chinese girl—most recruits were men—sober up, and start a happy family. *How disappointed were they!*)

Those epitomized the so-called losers in China.

Afterward, usually by the second semester, the ones that managed to stay resigned themselves to the experience—just four more months to go!—though complaints still persisted. Everything eventually fell into place, with about a month remaining on their contracts. (At about this time, some signed on for another year, which always puzzled Michael.) The next academic year the cycle began again and continued, until the next academic year, and on, and on.

China had become a landfill for America's discarded.

In April, the following year, Chen Hao stopped by to visit Michael. She had been one of Li Qin's roommates, and Michael knew her only as one of his former students. Sharing a bottle of wine, they talked late into the evening, and Chen Hao stayed the night. They slept together. In the morning, Michael made omelets, but was out of coffee. So, they had tea (Earl Grey). Afterward, they showered together, and then went into the city for coffee.

When they left the coffee shop, sometime around 3 P.M., Michael rode in the taxi with Chen Hao to the train station, and then stood in the waiting area to see her off. Her destination was Changchun, about a three-hour train ride from Harbin.

As the line began to slowly move to embark, she turned to Michael and said, "Li Qin is married." (He hadn't heard from

Li Qin since Thanksgiving, the year before. He wondered if she had already gotten married, but was afraid to ask anyone.)

Michael stared at her momentarily. He thought: Chen Hao must have known about us all along. Maybe everybody did. There are no secrets in China, he remembered someone once saying. But, he then said, quite matter-of-factly, "I figured she would be by now. I'd heard she was going to marry a family friend in Jinan."

"She didn't marry him. She lives in Paris now."

"Really?! I'm stunned. I'm . . . I'm impressed. Wow! Please, give her my regards," he laughed, nervously.

"I think it would best if I didn't tell her I saw you."

"You're probably right." They were silent for a minute, as they shuffled slowly toward the gate.

"She's with Serge now, Michael." He stared at Chen Hao in disbelief. Immediately, a flash before his eyes of Li Qin early that morning, the morning right after graduation, leaving the foreign faculty residence building; and then the conversation they had had in Jinan City, about living in Paris:

"We'll live in Paris, won't we Michael?"

"Anywhere you want."

"It's going to be so romantic."

She was actually talking to Serge at that moment! And . . . and . . . in the office, when Serge declared to be dating a Chinese woman and a beautiful Chinese girl—*ah, you're such an idiot, Michael!* It was Serge, after all. Michael now knew that he had been played all along. It took him a moment to gain composure.

"How's her mother taking it?" asked Michael.

"She went blind in one eye," Chen Hao answered, and they turned away from each other to hide their amused expressions.

Without speaking, they moved a short distance forward, and then Michael asked, out of courtesy or obligation, or maybe just habit, "Will I see you again?"

"No, Michael, I'm getting married next week."

Michael finished walking her to the gate, said goodbye, and then turned and left for home.

A cold drizzle began to fall as Michael left the train station. On the bus home, he thought about phoning Avery but decided against it. It'd be best to be alone now, he figured.

THE DIVINATION

MICHAEL RECLINED against a soft pillow. The assistant held the pipe over the lamp, and he drew from it. Then, slowly releasing the smoke and resting his head back on the pillow, he closed his eyes.

"Why 'Snake Woman'?" he asked.

"Tattoo," she offered.

"Oh," he said, and then opened his eyes to her. An oil lamp behind her shone a yellow glow around her top-knotted head, making it appear like a fuzzy lozenge, and he squinted to refract the light.

"You wan' looook-ah?"

"Why not?"

Snake Woman moved within inches of Michael, loosened the belt of her red silk kimono, and exposed her milky-white nakedness. The snake's tail began at the nape of the neck, wrapped around to the right breast, then below the left breast, then wrapped around to the small of the back, then wrapped around to the right thigh, and over to the belly and down, with its nose at the upper tip of the vulva. The snake was brightly colored, with bands of blues, greens, reds and yellows, and ovals of black.

"Beautiful," Michael said, and reached to feel the snake, tracing it from Snake Woman's right breast to the left. It writhed at his touch. Turning around, she allowed Michael to continue, until he came to the snake's nose, releasing a euphoric, orgasmic-like rush that engulfed him.

"Smooth," was all he said, as he looked up and into the face of Snake Woman. She hissed through a smile, and then robed.

Propped against a concrete wall, Michael awoke to the drone of machinery. He looked around. Everything looked different. It *was* different (*a boiler room?*). How had he gotten there? And, where was Snake Woman?

The room was warm and humid, and smelled of grease and hot metal. Water dripped from the ceiling, with buckets placed beneath to catch the drips. An old man replaced full buckets with empty ones.

Michael stood and looked at the old man. He was bald, scrawny, and very short, wearing only ragged shorts and sandals, and he pointed to a door. Then, Michael motioned to the door with both pointers, and the old man nodded. Michael took a step and stopped. He pointed again, for his own sake, and nodded. Stooping and focusing on the floor before his next step, he began a slow and calculated shuffle to the door.

As Michael made his way up two floors of concrete steps and out and into a narrow, garbage-littered alleyway, strays scattered and intermittent gusts spit a cold rain into his face. He slouched his shoulders, putting his hands into his pockets, and pulling himself into his core. It was late. On the street, traffic was light; buses weren't running at that hour. Without his phone, Michael had no idea of the time (he'd left it at home, so as not to be tracked). He walked the streets, until he came to a park. There, he stopped and sat on a bench in the cool, dark rain, and watched a large, lighted digital screen on the storefront of an all-night KTV (a club where people sing along to music videos) change colors and designs.

"Hello, Michael," said Helene, sitting beside him.

"Oh, you're back from hiatus?"

"I was never gone. So, how are you?"

"It's a little hard to tell."

"It looks to me like you're trying to kill yourself, Michael."

"I think I'm already dead," he replied, with a short laugh. But then he added, "No. I'm not trying to kill myself, just wasted that's all."

"Kind of extreme, don't you think?" asked Helene.

"Don't have the faculties to judge that, right about now," answered Michael.

"You're lonely, aren't you?"

"Lonely? Yeah, you could say that. But, it's not that I'm lonely for any one person. I think I'm lonely for the feeling of love. It's like everything inside of me is dead," he said. After a brief pause, he added, "I'm numb."

There was a long pause, and then he continued, "No, it's more than numbness. It's like I'm hollow inside. I'm broken, Helene."

"Do you have any regrets?"

"About Li Qin?—no, I've never regretted loving her. It's who I am, and I'm always going to be like that. I kind of like the way I am. But, I think I should forget about finding love."

"I disagree. You can be such a romantic, when you want to be. But, you struggle with it. It's like you can't accept that anyone could love you in return. You choose women that aren't the type to stay. You need to find love, Michael; *real* love."

"I really thought I *had* found it again—found real love again."

"What do you mean 'again'?"

"Like what I had with you," said Michael.

"Your love for me was conditional. As long as I was beautiful, domesticated, available, you were in love with me."

"Okay, point well taken. But, doesn't that just go to show that I *don't* deserve a woman?"

"Don't give up so easily. Remember, this is a journey you're on. When you've finished it, you'll be a different man. And, when that happens, a woman will come to you, and she'll bring you all that you desire. You'll know she's the one the moment you first see her. You'll know by her smile."

"Yeah, whatever; it's all irrelevant, I guess." Michael paused for a moment, and then said, "I think I should go now. I'm all wet. And, I'm getting cold. You should go, too."

"It's not time, yet."

"Why aren't you sitting on a cloud, playing a harp?"

"It's not like that; it's all right here: 'On earth, as it is in heaven.' I think I'm going to stick around, for a while longer.

It's just starting to get interesting. By the way, walk a block past the KTV, and you'll find a taxi," said Helene.

"Thanks. I don't think I could've found my way home."

"Yes, I know."

Michael stood up to leave, then turned to Helene and said, "Hey, want to do me a favor? The next time you see God, tell him I want a son."

"Will do, Michael."

Leaving the park, Michael walked past the KTV to a *da jie*, until he found a taxi parked beneath the halo of a streetlight, with its engine running but the driver sleeping.

He knocked on the driver's side window, woke the taxi driver, and said, "Heilongjiang *Waiguoyu Xueyuan*" (Heilongjiang Foreign Studies Institute).

The taxi driver nodded, and Michael walked around and got in. He checked his wallet, and pulled out a fifty: "Good, enough to get back home on."

In his apartment, Michael emptied his pockets onto the desk: keys, a condom, three Yuan in coins, a full pack of paper handkerchiefs, and a folded sheet of paper. He unfolded the paper. There, in cursive, but reversed (appearing something like Farsi), were indecipherable lines. Michael walked into the bathroom, and held the paper up to the mirror. It read:

Soon it will be time,
To turn around,
My little goret,
And come home.

"What?!"

It definitely wasn't his handwriting, and Frenchie was the only one that had ever called him "little *goret*"; but, that was all he knew. Folding the sheet of paper back up, he tossed it onto the desk next to the condom.

The condom; he looked at it; he picked it up. He'd only brought one that he could remember. "Oh, yeah, that woman—what was her name? Jin . . . Jin-something—Shan . . . yeah, it was Shan. Or, maybe it was Shan Jin. Why don't they have easier names? I guess I must have raw-dogged her . . . not good! Oh, but she probably had one," he said, convincing himself.

And, from his bedroom window, Michael could see that the morning sky was about to break.

"I won't come home, Frenchie, until my story is finished, and Maud is no longer in Crooked River," he said to the window.

THE ORPHAN

IT WAS LATE FEBRUARY, and Maud took Susie for her morning "constitutional", as she had done every day since Susie was housebroken, some six years before. The past few days were warm, melting the snow along the snow bank, and the edge of the road turned wet and slushy. But, in the early morning hours, without any direct sunlight, the road edge remained icy, from subfreezing temperatures the night before.

As Maud and Susie turned to make their way back, they heard a loud, mournful howl deep in the woods. Susie whined and fidgeted, and both began a quick gate back home. But, Maud slipped on the ice and fell backward. She hit the back of her head hard, and fell unconscious for a moment. When she gained consciousness, she staggered back to the house, entered the front door, and collapsed in the foyer.

Lois, a neighbor (neighbors were miles apart on that stretch of Crooked River Road), was driving by, when she saw Susie sitting on the steps and barking. Knowing that Maud would never let Susie outside alone—there were bears and wolves and coyotes (and the occasional spotting of a cougar), in the area—stopped to investigate. She found Maud face down, unconscious, but still breathing.

The ambulance arrived within 20 minutes and took Maud to the seven-bed community hospital, where she was pronounced dead within minutes.

Luc LeBlanc called Michael. Leaving China on the earliest flight, Michael arrived in Crooked River after two days of traveling, but only one day later. The funeral was civil, proper for someone like Maud.

(Maud's funeral was unlike Frenchie's, where wailing and war whoops drowned out the cheesy funeral home music. Auntie Zoe, Frenchie's youngest of eight siblings, arrived with one of her long braids hacked off at the scalp—she had used her son's hunting knife, on the ride over to the funeral home (why had he taken along his hunting knife to a funeral?). And, most of Frenchie's kin were inebriated and dropping to the floor, or occasionally picking fights with each other. It was quite a spectacle.)

The community hall was packed for Maud's funeral. She was well-known and respected in Crooked River, always quick to volunteer, to donate: a socialite, a saint in an Indian community, if there ever could be one; that was Maud.

Michael shook hands, nodded, and occasionally managed to smile. But, he wanted desperately to leave. Catholic funerals were too predictable, too sterile, too suffocating. He wanted the wailing and war whoops, the cutting of skin, the hacking of hair, drunken Indians collapsing, and drums would be nice, too. Now, that would be a funeral, a sending off to the other side, the proverbial walk across the log.

Slipping out the back door of the community center, Michael caught a ride with a group of teenagers, who were drinking beer, smoking weed, and jamming to Metallica.

Michael swigged the last of his beer, as a joint was passed to him.

"No thanks, I'm cool," said Michael, knowing that he might be drug tested, upon his return to China.

"Sorry 'bout your Mom," said one.

"Yeah, thanks," answered Michael, nodding.

"She was a good woman. Everybody liked her," said another.

Not quite everybody.

"Yeah, she's in heaven now, man," said a third.

Maybe. Or, one of the Catholic alternatives.

Back at Maud's, Michael packed the few belongings that he had brought with him, and then called Luc LeBlanc, who had left the funeral immediately after the service, and was on standby to give Michael a ride to Red Rock. From there, it was a short flight to Chicago, and then a long flight to Beijing. From Beijing, Michael took the slow train to Harbin.

On the train to Harbin, Michael had a lot of time to think of those in his life who had died. He thought of himself as an orphan now. Frenchie had died (accident), then Old Man LeBlanc died (diabetes), and now it was Maud (accident). But, how would he go: heart disease, accident, diabetes, cirrhosis, suicide? Michael wondered about his own death—when and how it would come. *Will it be today?* But, he didn't fear death. And, when it came to him, then he would know.

Classes at the university had already begun. He had to make up classes for the first week missed. For the first two weeks, Michael stayed busy. But then, it all fell back into his easy, accustomed routine.

THE DEPARTURE

WHEN THE DAYS OF MAY began to warm, and Michael could smell summer in springtime, a familiar restlessness stirred within him. It was time to leave China he knew, and now that Maud was gone, he could return to Crooked River for good. It was the homeland he loved: those areas, those sites, of hemlock knolls, surrounded by red cedar swamps; of maple, birch, and poplar woodlands; of spruce and fir stands; of old railroad grades and logging roads that called ruffed grouse to their sides on cold, bright October mornings; of native brook trout in overgrown streams and out-of-the-way rivers; of ruins of company towns from centuries past, where only broken chimneys, foundations, and well casings (and one flowing well) remained. The smell of autumn, of late autumn mornings, the sound of geese far overhead, on cold, snowy November days, migrating southward—those were all Michael's America, a synergism of experiences in sights, smells, and sounds. It had nothing to do with a flag. It had everything to do with his sense of place.

In China, gone was the marvel of everyday, simple experiences and pleasures, when he had first arrived, when he awoke each day with a feeling of anticipation. He had now become like other Americans, indifferent to it all. In place of anticipation were frustration and irritation with noise and crowds. On city streets and in shops and restaurants, smiles and inquisitiveness had become scowls and looks of distrust. It comes with development, reasoned Michael. Though, he might have only then become sensitive to it. And, China had gone crazy in its "pursuit of happiness". It had become like "dog-eat-dog America".

It had taken its toll on him.

(A French scholar once said that the real China existed 100 meters off of any major street, beyond a façade of modernity, where little had changed for decades. He was speaking of infrastructure and architecture, mostly. But presently, uncontrolled, rapid development had already advanced into the outskirts, into neighboring villages, swallowing up farmlands, the residents' livelihoods. KTVs were found in remote areas, in small villages. When and where would it all end?)

Before the craziness became intolerable, before he did something stupid, Michael gave in to his feelings and prepared to leave. Besides, his story was now finished, a work that would be memorable, when he looked back upon his time in China. And, he had sent it off to Loch.

But, there was much that he would miss: the garden-like campus of flowering trees and bushes, in spring and early summer, and the pond, where he had sat and listened to the quiet in the early mornings, while China slept, and nobody knew he was there. The quiet, little Mongolian restaurant he had discovered on one of his excursions, through the dirt backstreets of the city, where he feasted on his "usual"—fried mutton, shallot, and peppers—and always alone; it was his very own secret place. In the evenings, before the frigid winter months, women danced in a circle to drums, while fanning themselves, in a nearby parking lot (so familiar). And, young lovers who sang quietly, while walking arm-in-arm. *Wasn't America like that at one time?* That was Michael's China.

But, it was the freedom afforded foreigners in China (as paradoxical as that might seem) that he would miss the most: freedom from oppressive taxation, freedom from unnecessary and illogical materialism, freedom from the anxiousness that comes with walking city streets after dark, freedom to compliment a beautiful woman, without suspicion and retribution. And, there were many other freedoms, but mostly it was a freedom from worry, a simple, unencumbered contentedness—an easygoing existence. It was something he had never truly experienced in America, not since a boy, with Frenchie and Maud by his side in Crooked River.

In all, China had been a good experience for Michael. Being away, he had stood back and seen the big picture (*within middle ground, one can only see the immediate*), and now he had a different perspective, a more realistic perspective of America. And, he learned some realities of China that had been skewed by American institutions. Still, he had to leave.

Back in the States, Michael needed a place to live, a base camp to which he could always return, and someone with whom to travel about and share his adventures. He called Avery and they met for coffee.

Michael explained his plans and asked Avery to join him.

"Thank you, Michael, however, I must decline. My life is here."

"But, you could start a new life with me."

"Michael, I've already been to America."

"Then, you should know how good it could be," he answered.

"Yes, there are many good things about America. But, there are bad things, too."

"Like what?"

"Like anger and violence, Michael. And, it's all so random. America is distressed, so strangely afraid of . . . what's America so afraid of? Tell me, what's up with all the guns and so many mad dogs? And, don't tell me they're all for hunting."

"I guess every American is afraid of every other American," answered Michael, laughingly. But, he knew that Avery was right. Anything short of agreement would only make him appear foolish, naïve.

(The Crooked River Band reserved the treaty right to hunt, which was protected by the U.S. Constitution and international law. To prevent them from exercising their treaty rights was considered cultural genocide. Many members owned guns. Frenchie had owned guns, though they were kept *unloaded* in the house. Neither he nor Maude was paranoid.)

America had become desensitized, Michael believed. Media is partially to blame, a speaker at a conference once reasoned, and Michael agreed. Americans cannot separate conflict from their everyday thoughts and behaviors. It's as if society necessitates it. Without conflict, society becomes irrational, unrealistic, to an irrational and unrealistic mind. And, quite possibly worst of all, it's become so commonplace that society has become apathetic to it. It's in our films and literature; it's integral to American storytelling. Americana had evolved into a culture of violence. America desperately needed to find balance.

Avery continued, "Something's gone horribly wrong with America. It's as if violence has somehow become an option in solving its everyday problems! Why do innocent people—especially innocent children, who have their whole lives ahead of them—have to die at the hands of psychopaths?"

"I don't have the answer."

"It was rhetorical, Michael."

"You don't have to participate in *that* America," said Michael.

"But, it's everywhere, there, in America. Maybe, it's all the competition, the jealousy and frustration that competition brings. What's that saying, 'Keeping up with the . . .?"

"The Joneses."

"Yes, that's it: 'Keeping up with the Joneses'. But, isn't one person's success good for everyone?"

"It should be, but it never could be. Maybe it's the way it's always been, and it's as simple as that: it is human nature to be competitive, and competition leads to violence," said Michael.

"Okay, maybe in primitive man—mating, for example—but haven't we evolved beyond all that?" said Avery.

Michael knew it was rhetorical, so he nodded, as if in sudden agreement. Desperate for something, anything to convince Avery to join him in America, he asked, "Okay then, what about our 'all-American up-yours privileges'?"

"Pardon me?"

"Free speech," said Michael.

"Come on, Michael, do you really think free speech is limitless in America?"

"Do you mean like, you can't shout 'fire' in a crowded theatre?"

"No. What I mean is, look at the demonstrations that are quashed by police. The same thing happens in China, maybe every country," answered Avery, pausing for a moment, and then added, "But, of course, freedom to express one's views is important. In fact, it's the beginning of change, and change is coming to China. It comes slowly. And, it's coming quickly, apparently too quickly for some."

"Too quickly? What do you mean by that?" Michael asked.

Avery smiled and said, "Have you heard abou the poor farmer in Mongolia, who is now driving a Ferrari?"

"Is this a joke?"

"No, it's true."

"Well, Mongolia isn't China, is it? Are you talking about a poor farmer in Inner Mongolia?" asked Michael.

"Many Mongolian people still think Inner Mongolia is part of Mongolia, regardless of the flag flapping overhead," answered Avery.

"Separatists?"

"Nationalists," she answered. "It's their homeland."

Michael grinned. It was like some of the elder Anishinaabeg people in Crooked River, who believed and understood that lands and lakes could never be owned individually, or by some *foreign* presence. It had been bequeathed to the Anishinaabeg people to nurture and sustain, for the next generation, not to exploit and manipulate for personal gain; and, in return, the Anishinaabeg people were nurtured and sustained. It was symbiotic.

"Michael, what you are doing in China is important. You're giving Chinese people insight into a world they might otherwise never know. The generation you're teaching—'the twentysomethings'—is going to be the one to bring ultimate and lasting change to China, and I want to be here to watch it happen." She paused momentarily, and then added, "I love my country, Michael. And, because I love it, I want it to change for the better. I hope I can live that long."

"I hope you can, too," he said.

"I'm going to stay put, Michael," Avery finished.

Michael was dejected. Avery would have made a good companion, and he could have learned from her. But, there was no way to convince her to leave her home and start a new life with him.

"More coffee?"

"No, and don't look so sad, Michael."

"I just thought you would be thrilled to join me."

"I'm sorry. But, I *am* thrilled that you asked, really I am. So, why don't you stay here with me? It could be interesting, starting a life together in China."

"Do you mean: 'us, forever'?"

"Forever is a long time. Let's try it for a while and see what happens."

Michael sat quietly for a moment. "I hadn't thought about—

"Okay, then," she interrupted, "how about we go to my apartment, drink some wine, and think about it there."

"That sounds better, for the time being," answered Michael.

They stood up, and, as they started for the door, Avery turned to Michael, wrapped her arm around his, and said, "You may stay the night again, if you'd like." She paused and added, "My husband's out of town for the week."

"What?! You're married?"

"It's a form . . . form . . ."

"Formality?"

"Yes, a formality, a business arrangement, a mere technicality that can be easily changed and totally erased. Our marriage is open, Michael. In fact, right now he's in Shijiazhuang with his girlfriend, and now I'm here with you. How does that make you feel? Does it bother you?"

"Well, I'm not totally sure if I . . ."

Back in Crooked River, Michael rented a one-bedroom house in the 160 and planned his next move. The inheritance that Maud had left him, from her own inheritances (two trust funds, and shrewd investments later in life) was sizeable.

(One thing Maud had done, which was visionary, was sell her house with surrounding property, when the market peaked. The house and property had been paid in full, at the time of her purchase of it. The sale to wealthy investors from the Chicago area was under the condition that she would continue to live in the house, paying land taxes, utilities, upkeep, and so on, until her death or voluntary relinquishment. The profit on the sale of her home was considerable.)

Though Maud was always there to lend a helping hand, her policy—"self-reliance"—was to lift a person, be it kin or neighbor, to a point where the person could then begin to help himself or herself achieve independence. She wondered, though, was Michael different? Could he ever be self-reliant again, or would he forever need her? And, it worried Maud.

When Maud's will was read, Michael wasn't the least surprised by most of it. He had been informed beforehand that Maud had established a trust fund for him, and that it was "adequate", to say the least; that is, it was adequate enough so that he could write, and find that which was lost from within him. And, he made a list of things he should do, and a list of things he could do.

Michael had always wanted to follow the migration route of the Anishinaabeg peoples, from the mouth of the St. Lawrence River to the Straits of Mackinac, stopping at each of the Turtle Islands, from stories had had been told. From the Straits, he would pick up Peter Pond's route to the plains, and then head further west to the Prairie Provinces, stopping at Lake Athabasca. His ancestors had accompanied the famed fur trader there. The idea had come from Momaday's *The Way to Rainy Mountain*. But, unlike Momaday's most inspiring project, he wouldn't attempt to have it published. It would be solely for himself, something cathartic, and when finished he would revel in its completion. This, he could and would do. He had the time, now that he had the money.

The truth about Maud was known throughout the area and some believed it, while others didn't, but it was, nevertheless, the truth. Maud was privileged but too proud to flaunt it.

When Maud's father became the Chief of Medicine at St. Gabriel's Hospital in Little Falls, Minnesota, her mother, a former state representative (Republican), returned to homemaking. The family was prominent in the city, well-known throughout the state, and wealthy beyond the imaginations of most that lived in Little Falls and surrounding locales. In summertime, the family traveled to a summer home on Lake Michigan, about half way between Red Rock and Crooked River. Maud had always said that, when she was grown, she would live there or somewhere nearby. And, she did, surprising her parents and all others that knew the family well, by accepting a teaching position at Crooked River Public School, a K-12 rural school. Her parents figured that, after a year or two, she would either get bored there or come to her senses and leave. But such wasn't the case. In her first year in Crooked River, she met Frenchie.

Frenchie was at the school doing some carpentry—building coat closets, in the rear of each classroom—when Maud spied him. He was tall and slim, but muscular, with thick black hair and light green eyes. Maud was mesmerized. Frenchie had had other girlfriends, but not many, and none were serious. But, when he saw how Maud looked at him, he knew she would be his, much to the mortification of Maud's parents. Given the social differences between the two, Maud's parents soon likened it to a mission, probably a Jesuit mission, as Maud was a graduate of St. Benedict College. So, Maud became Sainte Maud of the Crooked River Anishinaabe, in their eyes forever after.

But, Frenchie soon died, and just in time for Maud's sake (and that of her parents). She was still relatively young and beautiful—fair, slightly built, of average height, very confident, determined, well-versed in the humanities, as her parents meant her to be. One day, while Christmas shopping and dining out with friends in Red Rock, she caught the eye of a recently widowed cardiologist. Within a year, they were married, and Maud left Crooked River (and the "ain't got no" crowd, as the famed cardiologist so fondly labeled the residents there), and moved to her new home. It was quite the "palatial estate" on Lake Michigan, just outside of Red Rock.

Fifteen years passed.

Michael was a young, promising assistant professor, married to Helene, when Maud phoned him with the news of the cardiologist's death. Given that he had been a heavy smoker, it wasn't at all shocking to Michael. Frenchie's death helped Maud deal easily with husband-number-two's death. She had loved Frenchie; the cardiologist, she had only considered a good investment.

The cardiologist's death, as with Frenchie's, was timely for Maud. She, now financially set for life, returned to Crooked River alone. She actually liked the "ain't got no" crowd.

Michael hiked into the 4-O-5, down the hemlock knoll to the old logging road, now flooded from the beaver dam (no one had trapped the 4-O-5, after Frenchie died), through the tag alders that had grown thick there, that eventually led to where Frenchie's trapper shack once stood.

Luc LeBlanc had returned to the shack, per Maud's instruction, emptied it of all gear and provisions, and then burned it to the ground to keep Michael from running away to it. The fire had burned so hot that even now, more than 30 years later, nothing grew on the spot.

Elders from Crooked River knew that the land was in mourning, so they brought tobacco to the spot, and prayed that the land would heal. It hadn't. As Michael stood at the edge of the burned spot, he also knelt and placed tobacco there. He prayed to his ancestors, for the sake of the land, and knew it would now heal—Michael had returned to his homeland.

Michael sat with his back to a large poplar, and thought about Frenchie. What if Frenchie hadn't died when he did, would Michael's life be different now? Would he have lived like Frenchie, by the seasons: hunting, fishing, trapping, pulling nets on Lake Michigan?

That world was Frenchie's world—the Great Turtle, where Crane beckoned the others to gather, and the ghosts of his ancestors dwelled amongst the living. The land and all its members—soils, rocks, trees, lakes, whitefish, bears, and all other living things—nurtured and protected its people. It was where the bear brought them medicine and knowledge in dreams. Frenchie's world was Michael's world. And when he—Michael—died, he *would* die there at Crooked River like Frenchie did, where he was supposed to die.

In the sun and a warm, gentle breeze, Michael shut his eyes, and tried to remember Frenchie's face.

THE CRISIS

FRENCHIE WAS LOADING his snowshoes into the bed of the pickup truck, when Maud drove up the driveway from town.

"Are you taking off again, so soon?" asked Maud. "You just got home."

"Ya, gonna set t'e Junction, eh—up t'e 4-O-5." Frenchie turned, and walked to the garage. She followed him.

"You spend more money on gas than you make from your pelts," said Maud.

"All you t'ink 'bout is money. It more t'an money, Maut."

"Okay, okay, but I need some help with these groceries," she said, knowing Frenchie was right, but hoping that Lake Michigan would break up soon, so he could set nets again. Then, he would stay put, and be busy for another season.

"Ya, as soon as I done loadin' up." He picked up a canvas pack. It was heavy, crammed with traps and tools. He walked back to the pickup, and tossed the pack into the front of the bed.

"How long are you going to be gone?" Maud asked.

"Oh, 'bout two weeks, I figger. Long enough, eh." Frenchie grinned. "We stay at t'e camp." Still grinning, he walked back to the garage, fully expecting an argument.

"We?!" Maud stood with her hands on her hips.

"Ya, t'e *goret* an' me."

"We've been through this before: the *goret* has a name, and it's Michael. And Michael needs to go to school! You just can't pull him out of school like this."

"T'e boy need t' learn t'ese t'ings." Frenchie grabbed an old wooden toboggan, and, flipping it under his arm the way a boy carries his schoolbooks, walked out to the pickup. Maud followed.

"No. He needs to learn school things. He needs to learn how to live in *this* world. Not yours." Her tone was patronizing.

"Go-to-'ell," he said. "You t'ink you so smart. So, educated white woman, what 'appens when you book-learnin' ain't no good no more? When t'e world, it become . . . it is unstable. An' t'en crazy peoples, t'ey in control. Michel be like e'erybody else: useless, weak, an' t'en dead. 'e need t' learn t' hunt an' fish an' trap. 'e need t' learn t' survive in t'e woods."

"You're paranoid, Frenchie. Bedlam is not going to reign any time soon. So, Michael doesn't need to learn your way of life, living from one season to the next. I mean, come on, think about it, Frenchie, what kind of life is that anyway?"

"A good life. Anyway, t'e boy . . . t'e boy 'e see t'ings."

"He doesn't see things, any more than you see things. You just want the company, don't you?"

"No, t'at ain't it. T'e Michel, 'e...'e ain't like t'em ot'er boys. 'e like me, eh. 'e need t'e learn from me not you school. Ot'er boys, t'ey c'n go t' you school. T'ey like you. T'ey like t' be 'round you kind o' peoples. Not Michel." Frenchie was pleased with himself; he had insulted her without actually calling her a name.

Maud mumbled to herself, "What was I thinking, marrying this damn Indian? Why couldn't he be more like his brother, Vincent?" Vincent was civilized. Vincent would know how to raise a child properly, she thought. She shook her head in frustration, knowing it would always be this way.

"I supposed he's already packed?" Maud stood with her arms crossed.

"Ya, 'e in t'e kitchen, eatin' lunch."

"What am I supposed to tell the school this time?"

"Tell 'em it none o' t'eir business, 'cause it ain't." Frenchie paused for a moment, "No, tell 'em 'e got t'e 'runs'. T'ey can't prove a t'ing."

Maud was stewing. She thought about it for a moment more. It would continue this way, if she consented.

"Okay. Damn it! Listen to me, Frenchie: I'm not losing this one. I'm telling him to unpack," said Maud.

Frenchie stood looking at Maud, like he was looking deep into her soul.

"Stop it, Frenchie! You know I don't like that look."

"You c'n 'ave 'im, t'is time, Maut," conceded Frenchie, as he finished loading his gear.

Maud was relieved. She sighed, and asked, "Help me with the groceries now?"

"Ya. Git anyt'ing good?"

"Nothing for you to take," she said laughing, but knowing too well he would have half the groceries loaded in the pickup before he left.

Frenchie carried the groceries into the house for Maud, and she followed, shaking her head, and chuckling mostly to herself.

"The runs," she said quietly, but loud enough for Frenchie to hear her.

Frenchie didn't return when he was supposed to, so Maud waited two more days before she contacted Old Man LeBlanc. Old Man LeBlanc was Frenchie's mentor in all things Indian (Frenchie's own father froze to death on his way home from the bar, when Frenchie was 11). He taught him how to hunt and fish and trap, and he taught him the stories he should know. Maud told Old Man LeBlanc that Frenchie was two days overdue, and that she was worried. Old Man LeBlanc was too old and sickly—he was 70 now and diabetic—to look for Frenchie himself. So, he sent his son, Luc.

Frenchie and Luc had grown up together; they were the best of friends, and the worst of enemies, always competing for Old Man LeBlanc's attention and praise. But now they were men.

It was 9 P.M., when Luc left his house in search of Frenchie.

Luc drove out to the quarry road and parked in the turn-around. Strapping on snowshoes, and, with a flashlight in hand, he began the three-mile trek into the 4-O-5. It took Luc a good two hours before he reached Frenchie's camp—a small, tarpaper trapper shack.

There was no smoke coming out of the stovepipe—not a good sign. Luc called out, "Frenchie!" But, there was no answer. He opened the door, and shone the light into the shack. Empty.

Searching the trail from the shack to the 4-O-5, Luc found only old tracks, maybe even weeks old. He followed the trail.

Before he reached the beaver pond, Luc spotted in the moonlight what appeared to be a log on the trail ahead. He quickened his pace.

It was Frenchie lying on his back, with eyes wide-open, frozen to the trail. Around his right leg was a loosely tied rope. Below the rope, frozen blood, and lots of it.

(For some reason, and a mystery to Luc, coyotes and ravens had left Frenchie's body alone. It should have been skeletal by then.)

Luc chopped Frenchie out of the ice-crusted snow, built a crude travois, and dragged him out of the 4-O-5.

When Luc arrived at the county sheriff's office in Red Rock, he told the officers his assumption as to what had happened:

"I think Frenchie was cutting (poplar) chips to bait the sets (holes in the ice), when he cut his leg bad. That big vein (femoral artery) is right there," pointing to the cut. "He bled-out before he could pull the tourniquet tight."

Luc LeBlanc broke the word to Maud a few hours later, and then Maud to Michael.

Upon hearing of Frenchie's death, Michael sneaked from home in the middle of the night and started walking. The following day just before dusk, he was found some 30 miles west of Crooked River, sitting on a deck of cut cedar and watching a herd of deer, with a few dairy cows, feeding on a pile of hay in a farmer's field. When the sheriff asked if he was okay, he simply said that he was, and that Frenchie had kept him company all along the way.

(Michael remembered very little from that time, except for bits and pieces of the funeral, and how Maud's friends acted so differently, so quiet, whispering, averting; whereas Frenchie's family was wild with emotion and spirit. Except for Vincent; always composed and sensible was Vincent. His heart was cold and hard, thought Michael.)

After Frenchie died, Michael's world changed drastically. It no longer made sense to him. Gone were the seasons, and he was made to attend elementary school every day. Though he was physically in attendance, he was mentally and spiritually elsewhere—the 4-O-5, where he and Frenchie trapped beaver in the spring, and fished its native brook trout in the summer; the Pie Shape, a triangular-shaped tract of land, where he and Frenchie hunted deer and grouse in the fall; Porcupine Crossing, where he and Frenchie picked blackberries (before the bears got them all), and apples in some forgotten homestead orchard in the fall; and, Makwa Creek, though he had only been there once, where he was told of his clan. It was a sacred site. These places he knew well, and knew what to expect of them, in any given season. And, it had been he and Frenchie together, always.

(As a boy, Michael was different from other children. An old soul, he was called by many elders. Through mostly observation, without asking many questions, he learned things from the natural world. The seasons had meaning, beyond the customary holidays and festivals. Places were sacred.)

Michael felt guilty that he hadn't been with Frenchie on the 4-O-5. Frenchie should've insisted on taking him along. He—Michael—should have insisted. He could have tied the tourniquet tight, and then gone for help. He blamed himself for Frenchie's death. And, Michael blamed Frenchie for his own death. He should have stood up to Maud. But, mostly, he blamed Maud. She had set it up to happen, regardless of intent, for the sake of his going to school.

Now, Michael was lost.

Soon, Michael became disruptive and uncontrollable. In turrets-like fashion, he mimicked the sounds that animals made, much to the laughter and cheers of his classmates (and, sometimes the entire class started making animal noises, too), to the chagrin of Mrs. Petit, the teacher. And, on impulse, he went to the window to watch the wind blow the few dried leaves on the branches of trees that had been too stubborn to fall, or a croaking raven on a nearby rooftop (*oh, oh, someone in that house is going to die*), or the distant flashes of lightning from an approaching storm. It was all rhythmic for Michael. It was like the sound of Old Man LeBlanc's voice, when he told Frenchie and him stories, or sang in that strange language, while the three of them skinned muskrats in the tool shed, on cold, November evenings.

But, worst of all for the class and teacher, Michael talked to Frenchie. (At that time, he began calling Frenchie "Frenchie", instead of Dad. It made the heartache easier for him to deal with; it separated Frenchie from the role of his father. Frenchie had become a person that Michael had known at one time, but was now gone.) It sometimes scared the children. But, Mrs. Petit was frightened all the time.

Mrs. Petit met with Mr. Gerard, the principal of the school, concerning Michael's behavior, and then they both met with Maud.

"Maud, Michael is too disruptive. I can't teach. And, if I can't teach, the children can't learn," said Mrs. Petit, matter-of-factly.

"Michael is one of the children, too. He deserves to learn like the other children. You should manage your classroom better," answered Maud.

"I've tried everything. He can't be controlled. He talks to your dead husband! Mr. Gerard and I both agree that Michael needs to attend school elsewhere," said Mrs. Petit, adding, quite condescendingly, "Maybe a special school, where he can get special—"

"I was thinking that one of the Indian schools up north would be best," interjected Mr. Gerard, "that way he could be with his own kind."

"He's white too!"

"Yes. But, he's an awful lot like his father," said Mr. Gerard.

"I know. I know. He's so much like his father," conceded Maud, and she began to cry.

Maud was at her wit's end. Not only was Michael disruptive at school, but also at home. He'd torched the tool shed, and had twice run away from home. Both times, Luc LeBlanc found him sleeping in Frenchie's camp on the 4-O-5. But talking to Frenchie, now that was different. What could she do?

Banging on Old Man LeBlanc's door:

"What's wrong?" said Old Man LeBlanc, when he opened the door and saw Maud's expression.

"He's talking to Frenchie, and . . . and, making all those, those weird animal noises. He's talking to Frenchie, for God's sake!"

"Michael?"

"Yes, of course, Michael. Who else?" screamed Maud.

"Get a hold of yourself, Maud. There's nothing wrong with Michael. He misses his father."

"It's more than that. He really, actually talks to Frenchie. He thinks Frenchie is there, right there with him."

"He is. Michael sees things. He's like Frenchie in that way. He's got one foot in the other world."

"He doesn't see things! And there isn't another world. There's just this world, this one!" Maud screamed again.

"If you want, I will raise him proper-like, like I raised Frenchie," offered Old Man LeBlanc, calmly and sincerely.

"You're crazy. You are all crazy, every one of you!"

Maud sped home, knowing she would get nowhere with the Indians in Crooked River. What Michael needed was a father-figure, a positive, civilized influence in his life, she thought. Vincent would be best for Michael, "Yes, Vincent!"

Vincent was Frenchie's eldest brother. A progressive Indian, an enigma, he was well-educated at a time when very few Indians were. Vincent, his wife, and two teenage daughters lived near to but outside of the reservation. They were Catholics.

So, Maud sent Michael to live with Vincent and his family. At that moment, Michael no longer called Maud "Mom"; she had lost the privilege of that title.

THE LIBRARY

VINCENT TAUGHT LITERATURE at the local college, and was chair of the English Department there. His area of expertise was poetry, most notably the American poets, and had an extensive and varied collection of publications, from *Voices of the Night* to *Leaves of Grass* to *Jacklight*, in his library at home.

Though Vincent's library was off limits to everyone— "And, I mean everyone!"—Michael sneaked into it many times, and for hours read poetry books. Once he was caught (he'd fallen asleep in Vincent's overstuffed chair), and Vincent beat the 'little savage' out of him, with a switch so hard that it left welts and bruises, and he couldn't attend school for two weeks. But, by then, Michael had already grown accustomed, numb to the beatings. It didn't keep him out. He was tenacious, and back in the library within the month.

The naiveté of childhood, of wonder and expression, abruptly faded. Vulnerable to and overly cautious and suspicious of imminent attack, Michael learned to show no fear and accepted it. Facing the threat head on, he fought it with submission. Approval, acceptance, appreciation, and love were unattainable. Criticism, humiliation, rejection, fear of abandonment, and feelings of inadequacy and inferiority were symptomatic and familiar. He became calloused. But, in the end, distrust spurred Michael to excel. He saw it as his way out.

By high school graduation, Michael's knowledge of American literature, especially poetry—early Modernism was his favorite— was exceptional, quite possibly unparalleled for a high school student anywhere. He was valedictorian of his class.

So, naturally, Michael attended university as a National Honor & Merit Scholar, with a multitude of other scholarships and fellowships. Most were national and prestigious. At university, he learned to be a white Indian, like all the other white Indians (a card-carrying member of the "White Indian Social Club"). He drank to excess—"See, look at me, I *am* Indian, drunk, I'm a drunken Indian, a freaking stereotype," anesthetizing himself, for the pain he felt of a life-way and homeland that had been "traded" for modernity and social acceptance. He fumbled ceremonialism and language. He learned "the stories" from the archives of the Bureau of American Ethnology. And, he said whatever it was that others wanted to hear: "spirituality; yeah, man, it's like . . . spiritual", and the all-important phrase, "Through education, I can be a role model for the Indian youth of tomorrow" (this one all Indians saved for scholarship applications). He stood or sat slightly stooped, with a solemn and somewhat Cro-Magnon like facial expression (knitted brow and protruding lips), and articulated mostly monosyllabically around other white Indians.

(The description "white Indian" referred to Indians that were either assimilated or acculturated in the dominant culture, or that appeared physically white. It didn't necessarily mean that they had totally abandoned all "Indianness". To many

Indians, however, blood quantum and/or residing on a reservation solely qualified a person as being Indian.

The question I ask is, "Would a quarter-blood raised traditionally by his full-blooded relatives or family friends on their original tribal lands be less Indian, in terms of Indianess, than a full-blood raised in New York City by adoptive white parents? That is to say, is culture less important than race?"

Race cannot be changed, within each individual. But culture can be. For the quarter-blood mentioned above, the boundary between Indians and the dominant society is clear; he's with his own people (and may speak their language), within their homeland, to which he holds a special bond. It's a fundamental relationship that he shares with his homeland: a land-ethic, a consciousness that he is a member, and that he belongs there. On his homeland, there may be sacred sites and traditional ceremonies practiced, in order to maintain balance in their world. It's tradition. Culturally, he is Indian. The full-blood, however, lacks it all. Blood quantum means nothing. It is an irony of Indianness.)

And, whites scorned Michael for being a white Indian, for his claim to minority preference. Their idea of being Indian was someone who owned a spotted horse, and lived in a teepee on a reservation. That was about as far as they were willing to take it.

Jumping to Michael's defense, Delbert Pretty Weasel, a Crow Indian from Lodge Grass (and one of a few non-white Indian students that befriended Michael), asked, "He's not Indian—why? because he's not on the rez, where he would be caged and fed, so he could practice those time-honored traditions of smoking meth and molesting children, is that why?"—to a group of Indian students that had called Michael a charlatan. (Most of them were urban Indians.)

The group wasn't amused. In fact, they called both Delbert and Michael racists and petitioned the university to have them expelled. The two survived the allegation, but Michael was forever after alienated. For Delbert, it didn't matter either way. His career goal was to simply return to Lodge Grass after graduation, where he would teach at the local tribal college. *Good for Delbert!*

But, Michael figured that all that sniveling would end once he was graduated. It didn't. There was little difference in the transition from student to faculty member, in that the alienation persisted. The only difference now was that, instead of students, it was his colleagues that were most vocal. He had to learn to defend himself. But, it was mostly to no avail. It seemed to him that he was always, somehow, being chastised for it.

"The only reason you received the Fulbright was because of your Native American ancestry," he had been told by a colleague.

To which Michael replied, "It's Anishinaabe. Don't be un-politically, politically correct." He paused to hold back his temper. Then, he continued, "And don't be jealous. It's really unbecoming of an academic. I *earn* awards, like the Fulbright, because I *deserve* them. I don't receive awards, just like I didn't receive my degrees. I earned them as well."

Michael had accepted the wrong teaching job from the onset. His academic dream job had always been a small, liberal arts college, preferably in the upper Midwest. Along one of the big lakes would have been most ideal. There, he could have taught a few literature courses, a few creative writing workshops, and disappeared in a veritable purgatory of academia. And there, in the mediocrity of it all, he would have written the perfect poem. He knew it, because he was capable of doing it back then. But soon, he found that only major programs were recruiting him. Why was that? Was he too good for small liberal arts colleges? Shouldn't that have been his decision? Regardless, it didn't happen. Disappointment was quick to ensue. Failure was imminent.

The reality of Michael was that he didn't belong in American academia, altogether. It wasn't because of any accident or death of a loved one (though, they had slowed him down for a while): he *never, ever* belonged there. Academia was different for Michael. He was different. His world was different. It necessitated balance, harmony. But, academia thrived in chaos, in argumentation. The two worlds were diametrically opposed. Success was therefore unattainable.

"Being an Indian student, and then later an Indian professor, only made for a stressful, very disappointing academic career. I snatched the dangling carrot, but it was rotten in the center. Really, all those years of education were nothing but a waste of my time and somebody else's money. It was a bad investment, all-around.

"Don't get me wrong, education does benefit some, but not all Indians—certainly not me. Those that can live equally between two worlds can benefit. Those whose families were assimilated and acculturated many generations prior can benefit. Those who became Indians in the 1970s, when it was in vogue, or when there was the promise of treaty money, can benefit. With all of these people, I really don't have a problem. I'm not judging them. Really, I'm not. They, however, would probably be successful *regardless* of their Indian heritage. And, when they *are* successful, it is an achievement not only for the student, but also for the policymakers that regard it as a true American success story. What I am saying here is that, for the rest, it can be a struggle. It can be disheartening. Success, by America's definition, is virtually unattainable for most. Is it worth the sacrifice? For me?—the answer is no.

"Employment afterward is problematic, as well. Graduates still face institutional racism outside of Indian country (*no, it hasn't gone away, and it never will*), and, in some instances, within Indian Country. There, in Indian Country, political power rests in families and clans, societies, and the like. Nepotism, graft, and discrimination dictate the hiring process, within the tribal landholdings. It's similar to how things work in China.

"The great experiment of educating the Indian for the past few centuries has, for the most part, failed. Grants, scholarships, and loans are irrelevant gestures of misguided benevolence. The consequential expectations?—sorry, America will never see a return on it. Indians will always be poor and dependent on the government.

"The only foreseeable way to eliminate poverty and dependence in Indian Country is to abrogate all treaties and abolish Indian status altogether. Open reservations up for purchase and development, move the Indians to the city, call them immigrants—after all, many moons ago, they had immigrated from Asia or Europe, whichever theory suits you best—and then group them under the generic umbrella of "America's poor". A change in definition can go a long way.

"Relax; it's sarcasm—sarcasm from frustration—in case you were confused or becoming agitated with me. My frustration means I still care enough to *be* frustrated. The alternative is apathy. And, apathy is cliché in America. Look around!

"If I had it to do all over again—and, believe me, I'm happy I don't—I'd attend college as a white student—hey, I look white enough to fit the bill. That's the big difference, going to college as a white student. And then, I'd stop at the undergraduate level. No, strike all that—it's all a bunch of bull. If I had it do all over again, I'd stay put and pull nets on Lake Michigan. That's what I was meant to do. Education only served to pull me away, further from my home. It broke the bond I had to Crooked River. But, that's where I belong. It defines who I am."

So, with his education then complete, Michael entered the real world of American academia, and found malice, deceit, sabotage, professional jealousies, and, most importantly, a desk where he sat and dreamed of being outdoors.

Michael woke up; the air was cooler, and the light was softer. It was late, late-afternoon, an hour or so before dusk. And still, there he was sitting against the poplar. But now, he looked around, trying to get his bearings. A beaver slapped its tail and dived.

"Oh yeah: the 4-O-5."

Soon, it would be dark and he knew that, without a flashlight, he would be lost. He had to hurry. He had become a stranger to his homeland.

THE APOLOGY

IN HER WILL, Maud stipulated one condition that shocked Michael: "Above all else, Michael must buy a boat." *How did she know?*

Struggling with the truth revealed, Michael headed off on a road trip to Little Falls, Minnesota: Maud's childhood home. When he arrived, he first stopped at a Perkins restaurant for a quick bite, and then stayed the night at the Best Western. The next morning, at about 6 A.M., Michael left Little Falls for Crooked River, taking the route northward to Lake Superior, and then eastward on WIS 13 to Chequamegon Bay. It was one leg of the route that Maud and her parents had taken every summer to Red Rock, and she spoke fondly of it often.

At Chequamegon Bay, in mid-afternoon, Michael pulled off the road, and walked to the shoreline. For a short while, he stood only looking at the lake. That day, it was so extraordinarily docile for Lake Superior.

And, in his mind, he talked to Maud, though she wasn't there and didn't answer him. He said: "Maud, you told me that it would be the good times that I would forever remember. But, that's not true. I don't think I have any fond memories, not after Frenchie died. Well, with Helene, yes; but, otherwise, not many. When I left Crooked River—when you *aband* . . . when you made me go to Vincent's—there were only brief moments of happiness for me: a teasing of what could have been, but never would be. I didn't want to deal with all that abusive reality. It was too painful. So, the life I created became a distraction, Maud. *It's all been a distraction!* I buried myself in all those books. It's no wonder I excelled. No wonder university was cake for me. And, I know you were so proud: 'all those awards', you would always say. But Maud, I think they were given to me out of guilt for the mistreatment of my ancestors, or maybe somebody else's. And, really, in essence, I was rewarded for giving up my true self. Education shouldn't be a form of cultural genocide. Why do we all have to be the same? Why was I so pushed and prodded? Why couldn't *I* be different? It all made my life worse, not better. There have been only shards of me for so long. I could see it, but nobody else could. On paper, I was one of *their* success stories—an American success story. And, I blamed you. I thought you were the enemy, Maud. But now I know you weren't. In the end, you could see all that. You *did* see all that—all the pain. You recognized the pain I had felt, in becoming that somebody that somebody else wanted to see; that you wanted to see. I'm sorry I judged you."

Then, he searched for and found a driftwood stick, and began writing in large letters in the sand: "Thank you, Mom."

There were no tears for Michael, only complete realization of who he was and where he belonged.

When Michael finished writing in the sand, he waited a few minutes for a wave to erase his note. But, it never came.

Michael left the shoreline and returned to his truck. It was a long drive out of Wisconsin and back to Crooked River. He arrived home late that evening.

DENOUEMENT: THE NOTEBOOK

PARIS

LI QIN SAT at the window, and watched the cold rain streak the pane. Pigeons cooed from beneath the eaves, and *d' Alesia Rue* was only a blur of hurried movements, and indistinct wet sounds. Her thoughts drifted to China, to Harbin and Michael, as they oftentimes did on those past rainy, mid-autumn days. It had been four years and nearly two months, since she'd seen Michael last: their five-star weekend in Jinan City. She opened *The Waves*, and began reading the same page she had begun reading twice before that morning. It would be difficult, Michael once told her, a novel in rhythm. But, she was determined to finish it.

She sighed deeply, and shut the book; but not today, she resolved.

Serge was off now, somewhere in The Philippines. He would return later in the month, or maybe the next. It was the schedule he had left her, and he hadn't called since his departure two weeks before. No doubt busy finding his next bride, thought Li Qin. But, she seemed not to mind too much, not anymore. Their marriage had become ironic—there was no love, only Sergey's all-knowing attitude, and kiss-less sex once a week. In fact, she enjoyed this time alone, her time to reminisce. Except for the rain, and the sounds because of it, the apartment was contentedly quiet.

She made herself a cup of ginger tea.

For some unknown reason, Li Qin recalled the time that she and Michael had traveled by train to the grasslands of Hulun Buir. It was during the May Day holiday, and Michael talked about the woodlands and prairies of his homeland. She didn't understand much of what he had said—things about horse cultures and woodland hunter-gatherers. But, she loved to listen to his voice, to the rhythm of his language, like the language of the open landscape, of the grasslands and the wind.

She missed his stories.

If it hadn't been for Brad, she would be with Michael right now, thought Li Qin. Michael had lost all trust in her, it was true. No, none of that would have made any difference, she then convinced herself once again. She couldn't see a future with Michael. He didn't have a future: a wanderer, a poet. But, what kind of future was she living now?

And, where was Michael?

"So, what's next," said Li Qin aloud, and lit a cigarette. Life had gotten complicated in Paris. There were certain expectations on her that she hadn't anticipated. She had matured sexually, for one thing—far too soon, for a Chinese girl. Sex had become tedious, pedestrian. She was merely going through the motions, but not all of them, not anymore. And Sergey grew restless.

Glenda, her orange tabby, jumped onto the window sill to watch the rain. Li Qin finished her cup of tea.

"I shall divorce Sergey," she told Glenda soberly, scratching her between the ears, and then walked to the computer.

THE CONFESSIONS

SLOWLY DRIFTING EASTWARD, the 20-footer rolled between long and gentle waves. The sky was clear and starlit. Michael sat in the still and fading darkness, waiting for daylight, and his floats to appear. Far out, the sky and the surface were still indistinguishable. Michael lit a cigarette, his thoughts drifting from one thing to another. Then, he thought about himself, and how he had changed over those past few years: he had become calmer and more accepting of things. The torrent of spring runoff had mellowed to a trickle of autumn. Michael felt settled and focused. He had succumbed. He was now nearly 45 years old.

Then, there was Li Qin. In the past, she had come often, especially in those quiet, reflective moments, but not so much anymore. Presently, she was there again, dressed like the last time he'd seen her—white sandals, knee-length, blue denim shorts, and a yellow sleeveless, cotton T-shirt—and shivering on the platform. Michael thought it quite odd.

Four years, had it really been four years since Jinan City? It had gone by quickly, he thought. And, it surprised him.

Was she still with Sergey in Paris? Three years of marriage was a long time for Sergey. He would be looking for another bride by now.

"What is wrong with you, Michael? Why are you thinking of her? You have Marie now," he scolded himself out loud. Marie took good care of him, and he loved her. Theirs had a future. He belonged in Crooked River, and she belonged with him.

"Four years," he mouthed.

And, then there was Helene, sitting on the seat before him, wearing a black Mongolian sheep hat. She recited:

Barren, she stood 'fore the window,
Music so soft, as the light that shone,
Rearing a child midst sorrow?
Knowing too well she would be alone.

"A quatrain, huh?" mumbled Michael.

"A message," answered Helene.

"Are you 'the bear'?" Michael laughed.

"No Michael, I'm Helene."

"I know. But, what's the message?"

"What do you think it is?"

"I'm not sure. Let me think about it."

Michael thought about the poem for a brief moment, and then said, "It's about a woman, who will always be childless, right?"

"Yes, that's part of it."

"What's the whole of it?"

"Barren here doesn't mean 'incapable of producing a child', rather '*not* producing a child'. There's a difference," Helene replied.

"Okay, I get it. But, this brings up a question that I've always wanted to ask you: 'Why didn't we have a child?' Our baby would have been beautiful—mixed race and all." Then, he laughed.

"Smart and healthy, too." Helene paused for a moment, and then continued, "Do you think it is wise to bring a child into a world that's so polluted? Is it fair? What I mean is: we're not given the choice to be born. It's beyond our control. This world, with all its greed and the stupidity that goes with it, is quickly being destroyed. We're approaching a threshold—a two degree increase in temperature—beyond which humans can't survive—at least, not as they do now. And, China's not the only culprit. The U.S. has to take its fair share of the blame—many countries, for that matter. You *are* aware of all this, aren't you?"

"Yes, of course. And, I agree with you: the 'me first' attitude has to change. Or, there will be nothing left, but an apocalyptic world." Michael sat quiet for a moment, reflecting on the greed that comes with wealth. "We don't possess the earth. It belongs to every next generation; that is, each generation borrows it from the one that follows. It's always been that way," he added.

"Yes, Haida philosophy, it's so true. The greedy oil companies—why do they continue to explore for oil? There is plenty in reserves. It's illogical."

"I know." Michael paused, and then said, "So, *that's* why we didn't have a child—global warming, huh?"

"No, not totally; it was mostly because I didn't want to have a child with you."

"Why not?"

"You were so distant, detached, forever gone to that mysterious place inside your head. I didn't want to raise another child by myself."

"Another?" asked Michael.

"Yes, another child—*you*." And Michael chuckled.

"But, you *were* pregnant once."

"Oh, you mean the 'miscarriage'."

"Yes, the miscarriage."

"Actually, it was an abortion."

"What?! Why?" asked Michael.

"The child wasn't yours."

"Not mine? Whose was it?"

"It was Andre's. We had sex in your office, while you were lecturing."

"Don't you think that was a bit risky?"

"Yes, of course, but that's all part of the game I was playing at the time."

Andre was sitting at Michael's desk, playing computer mahjong. Presently, there was a knock.

"It's open," he called out.

Helene stepped in, and Andre spun around in the chair to face her.

"Hi Andre, is Michael around?"

"No, he's teaching right now. He'll be finished in (looking up at the wall clock) about an hour, give or take. Is there anything I can help you with?"

"Well, I'm actually looking for my . . .", and she leaned over Andre, her breasts pressing against him, and began opening desk drawers. "I don't see it, anywhere," she said and then looked at Andre, their faces close enough to feel each others' breath.

"What? (*Gulp*) What are you looking for?" he asked nervously.

They stared into each others' eyes for a moment, and then Andre leaned forward and kissed her. Helene pushed him away, and walked toward the door, stopped, and then turned back to look at Andre.

Their eyes fixed on each other's.

A moment passed, and Helene sighed.

Then, turning back to the door, she hesitated.

She locked the door.

Walking to back to Andre, who was now standing, she stood within inches of him and whispered, "No kissing," as she reached between his legs and squeezed his erection.

"Oh," she moaned softly.

Andre swept one side of the desk clean of books, papers, pens, and the desk lamp onto the carpeted floor, and lifted Helene onto the desk, pushing her back, and lifting her ankle-length Hispaniola skirt to her belly. She pulled her panties down to her knees, and Andre pulled them off from there.

Quickly, he had his khaki shorts and underwear to mid-thigh, and penetrated Helene entirely with one big push.

"No noise," whispered Helene, through an exhale.

They worked it fast and hard, without making a sound, other than deep, forced breathing through their noses. Within a minute or two, Andre climaxed and withdrew. They both quickly got dressed, and returned the desk-things to the desk.

Helene started to the door, but stopped midway, then turning around she said quietly, but sternly, "I was never here, and this didn't happen. Keep your mouth shut, Andre. Do you understand?"

He smiled sheepishly and nodded. And, with that, Helene left Michael's office.

Michael had had his suspicions. After he had introduced Andre to Helene, at a faculty/grad student picnic, every time he mentioned Andre's name, she said something like, "Oh, he's so handsome," in that irritating, singsong, melodic way of hers, tilting her head ever so slightly to the left, and twisting and twirling her hair, through and around her fingers.

So, naturally, when Helene told him about her "scandalous" tryst with Andre, Michael tried desperately to recall a moment where he might have noticed a sympathetic look in someone's eyes, or even a smirk. But, he couldn't.

"I was suspicious," said Michael.

"If you were suspicious, then why didn't you ask?"

"Would you have told me the truth?"

"No. I would have denied it, and made you feel bad for asking."

"Then, why bother?" asked Michael.

"So, I would have known that you cared enough to ask."

"I suppose there were others, huh?"

"Does it really matter?" she answered.

Helene paused momentarily for Michael to contemplate what she had told him, and then continued: "You must know, Michael, women really aren't so mysterious, as most men think. We're purposeful and instinctual—yes, we really are. We see broad shoulders and narrow hips, and we are drawn to him. And, height matters too. It really does. Those things drew me to you, and Andre had all those qualities as well. I had a crush on Andre. I acted on it. I got pregnant. It happens: stimulus-response."

"Oh, the proverbial bell—"

"Yes, and I drooled. It really had nothing to do with you. It had everything to do with me," said Helene. She paused for Michael to ingest what she had told him.

"It—the abortion—was the right thing to do," she continued. "We know these things, after we die." She paused, and then added, "I had felt guilty about it for quite some time."

"Did anybody else know?"

"Becky did, of course. She thought I made the right decision, too. She was with me, Michael, at the clinic. She supported me. No one else knows. She didn't tell Loch, in case you were wondering." Helene then asked, "Aren't you going to call me a slut?"

"Slut? No, of course not; 'slut' no longer occupies a place in my vocabulary. So, are there any more surprises?"

"There's one, and it's an important one."

"Should I brace myself?"

"No, I think you'll be okay with it. Anyway, the day I died Becky and I were in a coffee shop, as you know. What you don't know is that I desperately needed to talk to her, and it wasn't about traveling. Becky was the only person I could trust. You see, Michael, later in the day, I was to meet with an attorney. I was going to divorce you."

"Oh, what a fun day this turned out to be!"

"I'm sorry; really I am," said Helene.

"But we'd just returned from French Polynesia. You seemed so happy with me there. So, was that some sort of a ruse?"

"No. I *was* happy. French Polynesia was absolutely perfect. I didn't want an angry divorce at all. I wanted us to be close friends. And, I wanted us to have that one incredible experience together that we would always remember and cherish. But, Michael, listen to me, I couldn't live with all the guilt, anymore. I needed to be free from it. I needed to be free from you. I needed to live an independent life."

Michael sat quiet for an uncomfortably long moment.

"Are you okay?" asked Helene.

"Yeah, I'm fine. It's just a lot of swallow all at once. So, why the confessions?"

"A couple of reasons: first, it's because you shouldn't think I was perfect—

"There's no danger in that now, Helene."

"Let me finish. And, our marriage wasn't perfect, either."

"Redundant."

"Michael!"

"Okay, okay, I'll shut up. But I *am* finding all this quite humorous. I mean, come on, I was so stupid, so incredibly naïve."

"Michael, you are only human. And, I was too. We act like stupid human beings sometimes. But, we learn from our stupidity—that is, hopefully we learn—and move on to become better people. That's what life is all about.

"I'm not asking for your forgiveness, Michael. But, forgiveness *is* a powerful thing."

"I know, and you're forgiven. What's the second reason?"

"The second reason: you're still alive, and you're different now, as well. You're where you're supposed to be, and you're doing what you are supposed to be doing. Look around: isn't this a scene from one of your dreams? Michael, it all has to do with awareness: awareness *of* belonging. The time had come that you could accept these things that I've told you."

Michael contemplated Helene's "speech of exhortation", and then asked, "What's with the hat?"

"Do you like it?"

"It's interesting."

"I was always too self-conscious to wear hats. But, now, it's like . . . who cares?"

"Well, to be quite honest, you kind of look like Buckwheat on *The Little Rascals*."

"Thank you, Michael. Goodbye—

"No, wait!—tell me, what is it like?"

"What is what like?"

"Where you're at, what is it like?"

"Michael, I—

"Really, tell me. I want to know."

"But, isn't life so much more interesting, when such things are left a bit enigmatic? Goodbye, Michael."

"*Aller avec Dieu*, Helene."

And, Helene was gone.

Michael continued his search for floats, and his thoughts flitted from Helene to Li Qin, to Marie, to children, and back to the floats.

"Awareness of belonging," he whispered, and then thought about Makwa Creek, his first trip there, and the vow he'd recently made.

"It was early autumn, and the salmon runs were on!

"One morning, hours before daybreak, Frenchie woke me up.

"'My li'l *goret*,' he said, 'I wan' t' show you a very special place t'day.'

"We had a quick breakfast of bacon, eggs, and toast, and then left home for the mouth of Makwa Creek. It was a two hour boat ride eastward from Crooked River.

"When we arrived, it was daybreak. Frenchie anchored near shore, and the two of us, donning our hip boots, waded ashore.

"Makwa Creek emptied clean into the lake. The landing, its surrounding landscape—the pines, the firs; its evergreen scent, in the cool, still autumn air—exemplified the term 'pristine'. There was no other word for it. It *was* pristine. I knew that nothing there had changed for millennia.

"The mouth could only be reached by boat, and few—only Frenchie and some elders—knew that Makwa Creek existed.

So, it was safe for the time being. And, Frenchie told me not to tell anybody about it. I didn't.

"I began to fish from shore, using Little Cleos; they're spoons. In no time, I had a strike and set the hook. The fight was on!—and what a fight. Remember, I was only a boy then. Frenchie sat back and quietly watched, as I fought the fish. I kept the line taught and drag screaming, until the fish was spent. Frenchie waded out to it—it was a Coho salmon—and netted it. The Coho was an average size male—some 9 lbs/26 inches, give or take—and Frenchie carefully removed the treble hook from its mouth—mumbling something that I couldn't understand—and then gently slipped the fish back into its home.

"By mid-morning, I had caught two more Cohos. They were a little smaller than the first, as I recall. After the third fish, I decided to take a break.

"At noontime it started to rain—not a hard rain, but a steady one—so, we took shelter under the boughs of a large fir. Frenchie built a small fire, there. Under those boughs, huddled together, we ate our lunch. Frenchie had made cheese sandwiches for us. When we finished eating, Frenchie told me the story of Makwa Creek.

"'Makwa was a traditional fishin' site fer our fam'ly an' clan. Before salmon come t' t'e lake, we (Frenchie meant multiple generations of ancestors) speared whitefish an' suckers 'ere. Makwa mean 'bear' in our language. T'at was our clan, t'en. No—not t'en—we still are t'e bear clan. T'is your clan, too, Michel. Makwa is a place you belong.'

"That was some 35 years ago, the autumn before Frenchie died. He died the following spring—beaver trapping, up the 4-O-5.

"In the years that passed—while I was gone from Crooked River—Makwa Creek was discovered. When I went there, after I bought my boat, the landing was littered with beer cans and bottles—lots of broken beer bottles and liquor bottles—plastic grocery bags, paper plates, tin cans, toilet paper, tampons, lots of cigarette butts, shell casings, and so on. You get the picture. In the middle of the landing was a large dugout fire pit, with the aluminum frame of a charred lawn chair in the middle of it. Makwa Creek—I'm talking the creek itself—appeared to be a dumpsite, as well. It was mostly bottles that had sunk to the bottom. Other trash must have floated out and into the lake.

"'Why would anyone do this?'" I asked myself out loud. To me, it was beyond senselessness. It had to be mindless, unstable people. Who else would think it was acceptable to leave the landing in that condition?

"Probably 'down-staters'," I told myself. But, then, I had to laugh. It had always been easy to blame them before; they seemed . . . I don't know . . . foolish to us, I guess it was. We called them 'beet-lifters', 'sugar-beeters', 'trolls', and probably a few more names that I can't remember now. They called us 'yoopers'. But, 'yoopers' became a source of pride for us. It identified us with the Upper Peninsula, the place where *we* belonged, not them. I don't think it was the same for the 'down-staters'—the names we called them, that is. Sorry, I digressed from the topic. The fact is anyone could have done it—desecrated the traditional fishing site—even someone from Crooked River. The elders are the only ones that still

remember Makwa Creek, as a sacred site. Only a few of them
are still alive. The young people don't care the least about
tradition.

I walked over to the large fir—the one where Frenchie and
I had taken shelter from the rain that day—and, yes, it was still
there. No one had cut down. Oh, that reminds me: in the fire
pit was a stack of blackened green brush; morons!—green
brush doesn't burn. Okay, back to the fir tree. I crawled
beneath the boughs, and gently brushing the soil aside with the
palm of my hand, I found some small chunks of charred wood.
They must have been from the fire that Frenchie had made.
Picking one up, I placed it in my cupped hands and smelled it.
Then, I returned it to the soil and covered it up. It smelled like
the fire that we shared that day. Olfactory memory is very
strong.

Here's the problem, Makwa Creek is on National Forest
lands. If it wasn't, then I would try to buy it to preserve it. As it
stands right now, I can't keep people out. But, I can keep it
clean. It was sacred to Frenchie; it is sacred to me. It's a place
where my ancestors had gathered, and it had provided for
them, sustained them. So, on that trip—my first trip back—I
made a vow to take care of it.

The first thing I did, the day I revisited Makwa, was I
loaded my boat with as much garbage as it would hold, and
started back to Crooked River. It took another trip to remove
all the trash from the landing, the creek, and the bottom of
Lake Michigan. I only went out as far as waist-deep, and I
didn't find very much. I think most of the trash must have
floated out a ways.

Makwa Creek is clean for right now. I think I got all of it—most of it, anyway. But, I know it's temporary. I will be back.

Off to the north, a half-mile or so away, were the headlights and groan of a tractor-trailer, as it downshifted to handle a stretch of curves along an otherwise empty highway. Michael finished his cigarette, dropped the butt in the baling bucket, and immediately lit another, by custom or character.

As the sky increasingly lightened, a bank of dull-gray, altostratus clouds to the west forewarned a change in weather. A storm was approaching, and Michael could smell it coming. As suddenly as the smell of moisture filled the air, a breeze picked up. The air turned colder and much wetter. The surface became choppy. He shivered, and then poured a cup of coffee from a thermos to warm himself. Steam rolled from its mouth and cup.

Presently, a gull lit on the bow.

"You'll go hungry today, my friend," he said to the gull. "By noon, this storm will be in Crooked River," he added. Knowing what to expect, he would have to clean his catch at home, lest he be caught in the storm. He would remove his net for the season, as well. He had stayed too long, even longer than Luc LeBlanc, and Michael's livelihood didn't depend on his catch (he gave away most of it to the village elders). For him, it was much simpler than occupation and dependency; it was ceremonial.

"Ah, there's one," he said, spotting a float, and then started the outboard.

HOME

BY 10:30 A.M., MICHAEL had already returned to his trailer. He had bought 20 acres of hardwoods (mostly maples) on Crooked River Road. The property wasn't far from where Maud had lived. There, he parked his new home, a fifth-wheeler. The sweet smell of tomato consommé saturated the already heavy, damp air outside the trailer. Inside, Marie stood by the stove: barefoot, in her pink, silk pajamas, stirring the pot and keeping it boiling, but not burning. A member of the Kettle and Stony Point First Nation, she was a white Indian, with striking Anishinaabeg features, but straw-yellow hair and emerald green eyes. Michael had met Marie while retracing the prehistoric migration route of the Anishinaabeg people, from the mouth of the St. Lawrence River westward to Lake Huron, then northward through Michigan (crossing into Michigan from Sarnia) to the Straits of Mackinac. A few miles south of Sarnia, Michael saw Marie walking along the roadside, with a gas can in hand. When she heard Michael's vehicle approaching from behind, she turned around and smiled big. *What a smile!* Michael stopped.

Marie had been clean for nearly six months, but it was still too early to be certain. It had been almost a year for Michael.

"You're home early, Michael," said Marie, still stirring the pot, but turning around to greet him.

"Yeah, a small catch today: three salmon and a couple of small trout—four pounders, give or take. They're in the smoker."

"Maybe tomorrow, a big, *big* catch," said Marie, optimistically.

"Nope, already pulled out my net—there's a big, *big* storm a-coming," he said, chuckling. "Still need to hang it, though."

"I'll help you."

Michael walked up behind her, cupped her small breasts with his big hands, and kissed her neck softly. With one hand, she touched her belly, sighed, and smiled that big, beautiful smile of hers.

"No need to help, Sweet-girl, I've got it. I'm going to check my emails first, see if my manuscript's been accepted," he said, as he stepped to the table, slid his accordion to one side, and opened the laptop.

"Oh, I almost forgot, Luc LeBlanc was here early this morning, and left you this little notebook," said Marie, while turning off the burner. She picked up the notebook from the counter near the stove.

"He found it in his dad's garage, when he cleaned it out yesterday. They're going to sell his dad's place, did you know that? You should buy it, Michael. We're going to need a bigger place pretty soon, and—

"The trailer's big enough for the both of us," mumbled Michael.

Marie giggled, and continued, "Anyway, the notebook's got your dad's . . . got Frenchie's name in it." She walked it over to him.

"You can say 'dad'," said Michael, as he opened it, and started flipping quickly through the pages. It was the lost notebook, the one in which Maud had written some of Frenchie's stories.

"*Gookoosh*—yes, that's it!" he said, excitedly.

"*Gookoosh*?"

"Yeah, *Gookoosh* . . . it means piglet," said Michael.

"Nah, it means pig."

"Oh, that's right," said Michael, still grinning.

While pouring Michael a fresh cup of coffee, Marie asked, "The notebook, it's important?"

"Yeah, to me—oh, sorry, I mean to you and me—it's very important." Michael leaned back in his chair and sighed deeply, contentedly. Marie looked at him inquisitively, not fully understanding how that dusty, old notebook could be of such importance to him.

Michael began to read "*Gookoosh*" out loud:

"*Gookoosh* left his place of birth . . ."

For there it was:

His legacy!—Michael's legacy, from Frenchie and Maud. Yes, Maud too. After all, she risked being called an ethnologist, if Frenchie had caught her recording his stories. In the notebook was "*Gookoosh*", a story to pass down to his progeny, and Michael could barely believe it.

"I'll check my emails later," he said, unaware that Li Qin's email was there waiting for him, and one from Loch, as well. It was Loch's critique of Michael's novella, now novel-length—"Instead of *Indian Time*, mate, why don't you call it *Anomie*"—with an accompanying job offer. But, there was still nothing about his manuscript of short poems.

Michael immediately began recreating the story of *Gookoosh*, from the incomplete notes that Maud had left, what little he could remember of it, and his own imagination and knack for storytelling.

Gookoosh left his place of birth, and journeyed far to find *naboob*. Soon, he came to a place, a very strange place, with a strange language and strange customs, and everything was crowded together and built upon itself. It was a busy place, and it was getting busier all the time . . .

It kind of sounds like China.

THE END

Acknowledgements

Special thanks to David Tenorio and Jessica Lockwood for their exceptional creative design for the book cover. It is how I had envisioned it. Good job, you two! For many years, I have lived abroad, and there have been those who have blessed me with their company. I would like to acknowledge some of them now: Elena, and her sons Valya and Kostya, Hughes, Suzanne, Adele, Helene, Cathy, Yolanda (Yoyo), Tony, John, Bill, Russell, James, and Michael. I thank you for your honest friendship. Last, but not least, I would like to thank my family. I love you all.

More books from Harvard Square Editions